Jewel of The Stars

Season 1 Episode 2 - "A New Reality"

Adam David Collings

Tamar Publications

Contents

The Characters   V

Previously in Jewel of The Stars...   VII

1. One   1

2. Two   8

3. Three   13

4. Four   20

5. Five   26

6. Six   32

7. Seven   38

8. Eight   44

9. Nine   49

10. Ten   55

11. Eleven   63

12. Twelve   70

13. Thirteen   79

14. Fourteen   86

15. Fifteen   94

16. Sixteen   100

17. Seventeen   109

18. Eighteen   113

19. Nineteen   117

20. Twenty   123

Epilogue   131

The Adventure Continues   133

Acknowledgments   135

Also By Adam David Collings   137

About Author   138

The Characters

Captain Les Miller. Canadian. Age 63. Les Miller has worked on space ships all his life. He met his wife working on a freighter. She always wanted to take a cruise. After her death, he transferred to Earth United Cruise Line, and has been captain of *Jewel of the Stars* for many years.

Staff Captain Maya Rice. American. Age 38. Maya previously served in the military. The long months away from Earth caused friction with her family. She now serves as Captain Miller's first officer.

Braxton White. Australian. Age 55. Former XO of the *HMAS Hobart*. Forced out of the Australian Space Navy under suspicious circumstances involving billionaire Dalia Spring. Recruited as Captain Miller's military adviser.

Jaylen Banks. American. Age 32. Security chief on *Jewel of The Stars*. Has previously served as a police officer.

Haylee Scott. American. Age 36. Passenger on *Jewel of The Stars*. Civilian astroengineer. Wife of Ronald, and mother of Elsie and

Austen. Currently in a coma after her heroic actions on the *USS Boston*.

Doctor Rashona Clarke. Jamaican. Age 45. Chief medical officer on *Jewel of The Stars*. Practicing Christian. Long-time friend of Les Miller.

Previously in Jewel of The Stars...

THE YEAR IS 2294. The passengers and crew of the cruise ship *Jewel of The Stars* are shocked by the news that an alien fleet has launched a full-scale invasion of Earth.

Captain Les Miller recruits passenger Braxton White, former XO of the *HMAS Hobart*, as his military adviser.

When Earth falls to the invaders, Captain Miller sets the ship on a course into unexplored space, but the enemy soon blocks their path.

Reluctantly, Miller agrees to a dangerous, plan led by Braxton, to steal a cannon from a derelict Earth warship.

Haylee Scott, civilian engineer and passenger, joins the mission to retrieve the cannon. She is wounded by an alien left behind from the battle. Now in a coma, her husband, Ronald, is left to care for their two children alone.

With the cannon installed, *Jewel of The Stars* destroys the alien ship and makes it out of Earth space.

Now, alone and cut off from everyone they knew, the passengers and crew must make a new life for themselves in the depths of space.

AND NOW THE CONTINUATION ...

One

Avaline stumbled down the corridor as the evacuation alarm blew away all traces of sleep. She clung to Daniel's hand. Her cold sweaty hand slipped, but Daniel tightened his grip. A sea of humanity pressed against them.

This was not the honeymoon she had planned.

"Move this way, please," a tall woman instructed. She wore a fluorescent yellow vest over her crew uniform. *Evacuation Warden* decorated the vest in thick black letters.

It had to be real this time. They'd had an evacuation drill just three days ago, so what was going on? Had the ship been attacked? Would the reactor breach?

People clamoured about, mostly obeying the instructions of the warden.

"This way. Briskly but calmly."

People crowded around Avaline in the corridor. She struggled to take in a deep breath.

"You okay, Av?" Daniel asked.

She nodded. "I'll be okay as soon as we're safe."

But they wouldn't be safe, would they? Other dangers would await them once they were on the lifeboats, adrift in space, with nobody to rescue them. Better to die here on *Jewel of The Stars*.

"It'll be okay, love. I promise."

"You know what they say about promises you can't keep."

"I'm serious. I made a vow."

Yeah. Till death us do part. That could be today.

A heavy metallic clang sounded as Avaline and Daniel turned the corner. A heavy bulkhead blocked the corridor. A warden stood in front of it. People started jamming together as there was nowhere for them to go.

"Could you all please turn around and go back. You need to use an alternate route. Wardens will redirect you to the next closest way to your muster station."

"Why can't we go this way?" Avaline called out.

"It's not safe. Please turn around."

What was through there? An explosion? A hull breach?

"What about the people who were in front of us?" Avaline's blood chilled.

"Just turn around, please."

"Oh, this is tosh."

"C'mon honey." Daniel tightened his grip on her hand and they started back the way they'd come.

A tear formed in Avaline's eye. How many people had they just lost? Were they dead? Were they being ripped apart by aliens? There'd been no reports of enemy ships since they escaped Earth space, but who knew what the crew were hiding?

She and Daniel were herded down a side passage, wardens directing them at regular intervals. Avaline sniffed and gritted her teeth. She had to remain strong. This was no time to fall apart. They could all grieve their dead later.

If only they could move a bit quicker.

She took a deep breath. *Just pretend you're in a crowd back home, trying to get on board the Tube.*

A throaty child's scream pierced the air.

"No! I'm not going."

As they drew closer, Avaline bent low to see what was going on.

A boy, nine or ten years old, was lying on the ground and shouting. "I want to go back to our room. I want Mom!"

Was this for real?

The kid was planted right in the middle of the walkway, blocking the sea of people trying to move down the hallway. A man pleaded with the child, yanked on his arm, while a girl, a little older than her brother, looked on with tears in her eyes.

"Come on, Austen. We have to move," the father said.

"No. I'm not going."

"You have to move that kid out of here," Avaline yelled. "We're trying to evacuate the ship. We could die here if we don't make it."

"He's autistic," the man yelled back. "He's been woken in the middle of the night by a strange loud noise, there are people everywhere, and his mother's in a coma. Of course he's gonna have a meltdown."

Oh! "You're Haylee Scott's husband."

"Congratulations. Why don't you help me, instead of criticising?"

Good point. This man's wife had risked her life to help them escape the aliens.

"Daniel." She nodded toward the boy and and took the girl's hand.

"Got it." Daniel took one of the boy's hands, while the father took the other.

"You stick with me." Avaline kneeled down to the girl's level. "My husband will help your dad with your brother."

The girl nodded.

"One, two, three." The men heaved and pulled the screaming child to his feet. Together, they dragged the boy along toward the exit while Avaline followed with the girl.

They finally reached a long hallway with airlocks all along the side. As they neared one, the door sealed.

"Next lifeboat, please." A female warden waved them along.

Almost there. Together, they all boarded the lifeboat. It was cramped. They wouldn't be able to manage in here for long. The boat filled quickly, then the door clanged shut.

Avaline's whole body tingled. Her heart beat out a dance number inside her chest.

Nothing.

"When are we going to launch?"

Daniel shrugged.

The boy banged his fists against the door. A few passengers gave dirty looks. The father grabbed his hands and hugged him tightly.

Another minute passed.

"This is getting ridiculous," Avaline said. "What are they waiting for? If this ship blows up while we're still aboard ..."

"Is it gonna blow up?" a nearby man asked, his eyes white.

"I ... I dunno," she said. "But they're evacuating us for a reason, aren't they? So either we've been boarded, or the ship is going to blow."

The man started banging on the airlock door. "Let us out! Please!"

A crackle of static filled the lifeboat.

"This is the Captain speaking. I would like to congratulate both passengers and crew on a successful muster drill."

Drill? Was he kidding?

"I know we sprang this on you unexpectedly. I understand many of you have probably felt a great deal of anxiety. Please understand it was important to see how you would manage under as realistic circumstances as possible."

Avaline shook her head and formed fists. She'd give the captain a piece of her mind if she had to tear the bridge door off its hinges with her bare hands.

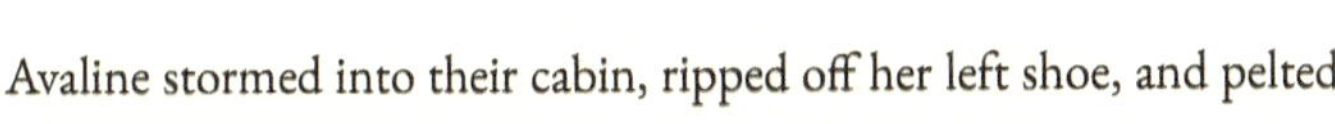

Avaline stormed into their cabin, ripped off her left shoe, and pelted it at the closing door.

"Whoa, easy there," Daniel said, gently putting his arm around her.

She ripped herself out of his grip. "Don't, Daniel."

"It's okay. We're safe. Everything is fine."

She spun and stared him down. "Everything is not fine. None of this is fine." She waved her arms about, indicating their cabin. "This isn't what it was supposed to be like."

"Look, I'll admit this was poor judgement on the captain's part but …"

"Poor judgement? Is that all you can say? He dragged us up in the middle of the night, made us all think we were going to die, then told us it was all a practical joke."

"Hardly a joke, love."

She pointed her finger at Daniel. "He had no right to do this."

"He's just trying to keep us alive."

"People could have died from heart attacks. Look what the Scott family went through with Austen. We've just been through a drill. Why'd he have to pull another one so soon?"

"I dunno. I guess he wanted to see if we had learned from the last one."

"And what's gonna happen next time? Hasn't he ever heard of the boy who cried wolf? I'd like to go up to that bridge and kick him in the—"

"Okay, Av. I get it. You're angry. I'm not too happy either, but getting worked up like this won't help anything, will it?"

She took a deep breath. "I suppose not."

"If it makes you feel any better, you can lodge a formal complaint. I guarantee you won't be the only one."

She nodded. "I will."

Daniel took a step forward and reached for her hand. His fingers intertwined with hers, alternating colours like the keys on a piano. His hands were warm. Strong.

"Now, since we're awake, and I doubt we'll be settling back to sleep anytime soon ..." He reached up with his other hand and undid her top button.

She locked eyes with him. "Are you serious?" Her blood still boiled with rage at the captain. She wanted to punch someone, not make love.

He shrugged. "Well this *is* our honeymoon."

"Just hold those horses, mister." Avaline held up a hand and took a deep breath. Then another. And another.

Daniel was right about one thing. This was their honeymoon. Something she'd dreamed about for years. Nobody was going to ruin it. Not even Captain Miller. She glanced at her husband. Her husband. Stars, she loved calling him that. He looked pretty good, all rugged and dishevelled from their ordeal. He'd always had that knack for extinguishing the fires in her heart with that charming demeanour. Well, and stoking fires of a different kind.

Daniel started to hum. *Nobody But You*, by Saturn's Heart. The first song they ever danced to.

He was right about one other thing. They wouldn't be getting back to sleep anytime soon.

She took another deep long breath and let it out. Then she grabbed Daniel's head and pulled him into a kiss.

Two

MAYA DROPPED INTO THE chair opposite Captain Les Miller's desk. How could he look so rested after the night they'd just had?

"Morning, Staff Captain," the captain said.

"Surprise drill last night."

"Yes. Everybody did remarkably well. We even introduced a simulated hull breach which forced one group to use an alternate route."

"I bet you're unpopular this morning. You sure it was a good idea to handle it the way you did?"

"It was Braxton's idea, but I agreed. The first drill was a teaching exercise to reinforce what they have to do, should we need to abandon ship. Last night was a test. We had to know if the crew could handle an evacuation, should we encounter the aliens again. Now we know."

"I can see Braxton all over this. Drills are standard practice on a military ship, but he needs to remember this is a ship full of tourists. They won't thank you for scaring them half to death in the middle of the night."

"Better scared than dead."

"Look at you all buddy-buddy with Braxton." Maya grinned. "Even following his advice. You've come a long way, Captain."

Les leaned back in his chair. "End of the world can do that, I guess."

Maya reached down, tapped her wristband and swiped down a list of messages, projected by her eye lenses. Several departmental reports, and another from Spring.

"I've had more requests from Dalia Spring to meet with you."

Les grimaced. "I guess I can't put it off any longer. Funny how even after Earth has fallen to invaders, we still feel the need to pander to a billionaire. Book her in for an appointment tomorrow."

"As you wish." Maya remained in her seat, fiddling with her wristband. Should she bring *it* up now or wait for a better time?

"Was there anything else, Maya?"

Here goes. Maya leaned forward, her mouth suddenly dry. "Yes, Captain. I'd like to propose a supply mission."

Les raised an eyebrow. "Go on."

"There's an abandoned colony just inside Earth-controlled space. It's likely to have—"

"Well, well. It looks like I'm not the only one who's been listening to Braxton's advice."

"He is our military adviser. Sir."

"The answer is no. I will not condone going back into Earth space."

"I'm not suggesting we take *Jewel of The Stars*, Captain. Just a small team in the shuttle. It's warp powered so ..."

The captain stood and paced his office, biting his bottom lip. "I don't know, Maya. It's a high-risk proposition. You draw the attention of the aliens the minute you go back into Earth space. Not only is the shuttle likely to be destroyed, but it will bring us to the attention of our enemies. They could trace the shuttle back to us."

"Captain, I doubt our enemies have just forgotten about us. If they wanted to, they'd be tracking us."

"Maybe. But this would make it certain. We do need to find supplies, and I'll keep this plan in mind, but I'm not ready to commit to it. We're not desperate enough. Not yet."

"What happened to all those changes you said you were making?"

"They just reached their limit."

"Very well." Maya turned and left the office.

Maya strode down the plain grey hallway toward her quarters. All the hallways looked alike here on the crew decks. She hadn't really expected Les to go for her plan, but she'd been hopeful.

Miller had always had a problem with risk, but he'd made so much progress in the last week. He was less married to the rulebook. Who knew—maybe this time he was right.

"Staff Captain?" There was no mistaking the Australian accent.

She glanced over her shoulder. "Braxton." He loomed over her, his bald scalp shining in the harsh hallway lighting. She turned around to face him.

"Have you met with the captain?"

"He said no."

Braxton smiled. "Predictable. So what's our next step?"

"No next step. The captain has made his decision."

"Yes, but he's been known to change his mind. We just need to show him his decision is wrong."

Maya gazed at her feet. "Maybe."

"What's up?"

"I dunno. It's just … this whole situation. I don't know what we should be doing. There are no guidelines for any of this. Are we certain the captain *is* wrong?"

"I am, but it sounds like you have your doubts."

"Doubts are all I have."

Braxton nodded. "Okay."

"That's it?"

"Not at all, but I now see it's not just Miller I have to convince."

Maya gave a fake smile. Braxton meant well but he could be way too pushy. "Have a good day, Braxton."

He nodded, turned, and strode back down the hallway.

Maya walked the last few steps to the door of her cabin and swiped her finger over the plate. The door slid open. She walked through, and it swished closed behind her.

She glanced at the time display in the corner of her vision. It was Crystal's day off, so she might still be asleep, but it was worth a try. She placed the call. It connected—audio only.

"Mom, it's early. I could have been asleep."

"You weren't, though."

"No. Somebody thought it would be a good idea to drag us all out of bed at an insane hour. I couldn't get back to sleep after that. Your idea, by any chance?"

"Not exactly, but the drills are important."

"Yeah, whatever. What you want?"

"Well, seeing as you have a day off, I thought maybe we could …"

"I volunteered to help out at work today. I'm going in for the afternoon, so I need to get ready soon."

Maya frowned. "Um … okay. Sweetheart, the main reason I suggested you come and work on board was so we could spend some time together. I pulled a lot of strings to get you this job."

"Yeah, and the only reason I came is because you and Dad ganged up on me."

"Crystal ..."

"I'm sorry, but I can't see you today. I have to work. You of all people know what that's like."

The call clicked off.

Maya flopped onto the bed and planted her face in her hands. Were all teenagers this difficult? Why did Crystal have to be so hurtful? Maya wiped a tear from her cheek. The worst part? Crystal was right. Maya's work had kept her from spending time with her daughter too often when she was younger. And her husband. By the time she'd done something about it, it had been too late to save her marriage. She wouldn't lose her daughter as well.

Three

Jaylen Banks yawned as he surveyed the kitchen. Between the drill and the nightmares, he'd barely got a wink last night. The room was a jungle of stainless steel made even more jungle-like by the bowls and implements scattered over the floor. He pushed away his fatigue. There was a theft to investigate.

He tapped his wristband and selected his note-taking app, then locked eyes with the chef who was fidgeting with his apron.

"Take me through what happened."

"Not a lot to say. I weren't 'ere at the time. My sous chef caught 'em in the act. Had pillowcases. They were stuffing food into 'em. Soon as she saw 'em, they nicked off."

"Any distinguishing features?"

"Not that anyone could tell. They had pillowcases over their heads, didn't they?"

"Okay, so pillowcases to store the food in, and but also worn as masks." Jaylen typed on a virtual keyboard. "Sounds like they have access to a good supply."

"You're gonna catch 'em right? Can't 'av people taking the food for 'emselves. Gotta maintain order 'round here, or people will starve."

"We'll catch them, but I do need to speak with your sous chef. Is she here?"

"Nah. Gave 'er the morning off, didn't I."

"That's fine. I'll catch up with her later."

Jaylen's wristband trilled with an incoming call. "Excuse me."

He swiped his finger in the air to accept the call. "Security Chief Banks."

"Jaylen, it's Rashona."

"What can I do for you, Doctor?"

"Sickbay has been pillaged."

Jaylen couldn't stifle a chuckle. "Pillaged?"

"I've just come in this morning. It's a real mess."

"I'm on my way."

He ended the call. Two robberies of vital supplies in one night. Things were getting out of control. Jaylen shifted from one foot to the other. As Chief of Security, this looked bad for him.

"What about the food?" Chef asked.

"I'll be in touch. We'll stamp this out."

Jaylen walked out of the kitchen and down the hallway. Sickbay was one deck up. Rather than wait for the elevator, he bounded up the steel stairs, two at a time. He was energised despite his mental fatigue. His fight-or-flight response, kicked into gear by his latest nightmare, was still very much active.

Looting had been an inevitable problem since they left their prescribed course and set off into unexplored space, but it had escalated much quicker than he'd expected.

Jaylen neared the door to sickbay. Three minutes and not even puffed. Jaylen smiled. His fitness level hadn't dropped since his days in the police force. He'd never regretted the career change. Surrounding himself with violent crime had been no way to live.

He stepped into sickbay. The floor was littered with bandages, swabs, and instruments. Many of the drawers hung open.

The instruments could be sterilised again, but a lot of the items would have to be disposed of.

Shelves lined all the available wall space. There were several chairs in a waiting area near the door. A desk, bed and chair filled the middle of the room. There were two doors in the far wall-the ward and a small operating room.

The ward door opened and Doctor Rashona Clarke stepped out. The large Jamaican woman lacked her customary cheerfulness.

Sickbay's ward was usually empty, but it currently housed the unconscious Haylee Scott.

"Is Haylee okay?"

"As okay as she was yesterday. Still in an induced coma, but stable." Her eyebrows drew together. "I haven't seen Bonnie."

"Bonnie?"

"Nurse Ranford. She was here on duty last night. Mrs Scott requires regular observation, so I always have somebody here to keep a close eye on her."

"How long have you been here?" Jaylen asked.

"I just arrived. I called you the moment I stepped in and saw the mess. I thought Bonnie would be in with Haylee."

"What about in there?" Jaylen gestured toward the door to the operating room.

"That was going to be the next place I looked."

Jaylen stepped over the mess and reached the door first, but it didn't open as it was keyed for medical personnel. As Rashona stepped up next to him, the door slid open.

Rashona gasped from behind him. A young white woman wearing pale blue scrubs lay on the floor. Several spots of blood stained the hard plastic floor next to her head.

"Bonnie!" Rashona pushed Jaylen out of the way and felt the nurse's neck. "She's alive."

Jaylen let out a huge breath. The woman was so young.

Rashona checked Ranford's vitals.

"She's got a head wound. No other signs of trauma." Rashona glanced at Jaylen over her shoulder. "Help me get her up on the bed."

Jaylen knelt and put one arm under Ranford's legs, the other under the small of her back. Rashona held her shoulders.

They lifted together and placed Nurse Ranford gently on the bed. She groaned a little.

Jaylen backed out of the operating room, giving Rashona room to work.

He swiped his finger along his wristband, looked at the mess and snapped a few images straight from his eye-lenses to the ship's cloud network.

"How's she doing, Doctor?" Jaylen stepped back into the operating room.

"She's obviously concussed. Has probably been unconscious for some time. I'm worried about subdural hematoma."

"When will she be able to answer questions?"

"Not for a while." Rashona shone a penlight in Ranford's eyes. "Even then, she may not remember much about what happened immediately prior to the attack."

Jaylen's fists balled. Ranford was attractive, apart from the blood matting her hair. What kind of person did a thing like this? Stealing food and medicine was one thing. People were scared. They didn't want to go without the basics, but to attack an innocent young woman? A woman who spent her life caring for others?

"This attack was inexcusable," Rashona said. "I tell you, if I weren't a God-fearing woman, I'd have a few plans for whoever did this."

"Then it's probably a good thing you believe in forgiveness. Last thing we need around here is vigilante justice."

Jaylen stepped back, tapped his wristband, then swiped down the security viewer and scrubbed to the time of the attack.

One man stood by the supply bench. His head was covered with a pillowcase, just like the kitchen thieves. Was that a coincidence?

The hooded man pulled at the drawers, but they wouldn't budge. The ward door opened, Nurse Ranford stepped out, and there was an animated discussion. If only the security system recorded audio. The man grabbed Ranford by the upper arm and dragged her to the bench. She opened the drawer for him, and he rifled through the contents.

Ranford reached for her wristband. The hooded attacker slapped her hand away from the band. He pushed her backwards, pointed his finger and shouted. Ranford hugged her arms around herself.

Jaylen's muscles quivered as the image of Ranford pressed her back hard up against the wall.

Suddenly, Ranford ran for the operating room, touching the plate to open the door. It was a good idea. She could lock herself in there and the attacker wouldn't be able to reach her. But he squeezed in after her before the doors could close.

Jaylen switched to the OR camera as the attacker struck Ranford in the head. She went down.

Jaylen's palms were slick. He'd seen all he needed to see. He tapped his wristband.

"Call Staff Captain Maya Rice."

Moments later Maya's voice sounded in his ears. "Jaylen?"

"Could you meet me in sickbay, Ma'am? I've responded to two cases of looting this morning, and they've turned violent."

Maya's eyes grew wide as she entered sickbay. A nurse lay on the bed. Doctor Clarke was taking her blood pressure.

Jaylen stepped forward as Maya walked in.

"According to access logs, it happened 4:32 AM, after the evacuation drill. Passengers would have returned to their rooms by then. A single intruder wearing a mask. Nurse Ranford was on duty. The intruder assaulted her and forced her to open the drawers with her fingerprint. Then the intruder knocked her out and left her in the operating room."

"What about Haylee Scott?" Maya gestured toward the small ward.

"They didn't go in there. Mrs Scott was undisturbed." Clarke replaced the blood pressure cuff.

Maya placed a hand on Ranford's shoulder. "Don't worry. We'll catch the guy who did this. Doctor Clarke will take good care of you."

She stepped away from the bed. Jaylen followed.

"It's been an eventful night between this and the theft of the foodstuffs, not to mention the evacuation drill," Jaylen said.

"People are scared." Maya came to a stop and adopted a loose posture. "We're out here on our own with limited supplies. People are going to take what they think they need."

"I think it's more than that, Ma'am. An ordinary person running scared isn't likely to assault someone like this. We're not at that level of desperation. Yet."

"You have to recover those supplies," Clarke said. "We can't afford to lose medications. People are going to suffer without them."

"What are you thinking, Jaylen?"

"I don't know yet. I need to investigate more. Nurse Ranford is in no state to be questioned right now. Maybe in a little while."

"We need to stamp this out now, before the ship descends into anarchy. Otherwise we'll never regain control."

"I'm not sure my security force is gonna be big enough. Not for this."

Maya nodded. "I'll take it to the captain."

Four

Avaline grabbed Daniel's hand. They swung their arms in unison as they strolled down the corridor.

"Do you think they'll be serving lunch yet?" she asked.

"I hope so. After missing breakfast, I'm starved."

"And whose fault is that?" She jabbed her elbow into Daniel's side. "Somebody wanted to make love in the middle of the night."

"It certainly cheered you up." He winked. "Besides, you like sleeping in."

"On the rare occasions I get the opportunity." She leaned in close and laid her head on Daniel's shoulder as they walked.

"Does this mean you forgive the captain?"

"No way. I'll avenge myself on him if it takes my dying breath." She giggled.

"I wouldn't want to be in his shoes, especially now you're a barrister."

"Junior barrister," she said. "I'm still annoyed about the drill, but I'm not gonna let it spoil my day. You're only a newly-wed once right?"

"Well, hopefully."

"Hey!" She straightened herself and jabbed him again.

Daniel smiled, leaned over, and kissed her behind the ear as they entered the main dining room.

"Welcome, sir. Madam." A waiter nodded to them in turn. "Are you looking for an early lunch?"

"If that's possible."

"Of course."

The waiter led them past the little fountain to a table for two near a porthole. They sat and gave their drink orders. The waiter was gone in a blink.

Avaline gazed out at the stars. Such a romantic view at any time of day. She called up the menu. Her eye lenses projected only two items into her field of view. Fish with salad, or spaghetti Bolognese.

"Not a whole lot of choices," she said.

"Well, they gotta ration the food to make it last, I guess." Daniel shrugged.

Avaline dismissed the menu and looked back out the window. Why did people have to keep reminding her of their situation. Couldn't they just let her enjoy her honeymoon?

"Av? What's wrong?" Daniel touched the back of her hand.

She took a deep breath. "Nothing. It's fine." She shook the feelings off. "I'm going to have the fish."

The waiter returned with their drinks. They both ordered the fish and were alone again. Soft piano music played in the background.

Something touched Avaline's foot. She glanced a look at Daniel. A wide grin covered his face.

"Are you playing footsies, Mr Barrett?"

He nodded, still grinning.

"That's not very mature."

She slipped her foot out of her shoe and ran it up and down the front of his lower leg, showing him a grin of her own.

"Excuse me," an unfamiliar voice said.

Avaline whipped her gaze to the left as she pulled her foot back.

A woman with short-cropped greying hair stood next to their table. She extended her hand. "I'm Olivia."

Avaline's mouth dropped open. The impertinent old ...

"I'm Daniel. This is my wife, Avaline."

"Can we do something for you?" Avaline glared at Olivia.

"No. I just wanted to meet you. I think it's important, given our current circumstances. People tend to keep to themselves on a holiday, but ... Well, this isn't a holiday anymore, is it?"

It could be if old hags didn't stick their noses into other people's business. Okay, maybe hag was a little unfair. She wasn't unattractive for her age—probably early sixties—but seriously?

"I've thought a lot about this." Olivia grabbed a chair from a nearby table and sat.

How long was she planning on staying?

"We need to come together. Build a community. I thought the first step might be to start getting to know people and helping them get to know each other."

Daniel nodded. "That actually makes sense."

"So what part of England are you two from?"

"London," Daniel said.

Why was he engaging with this woman?

"Ah, beautiful city. I'm from Novia Scotia."

"We've never been to Canada, but we'd like to some ..." Daniel's voice drifted off. "Well, I guess that's not likely now."

"Olivia," Avaline said. "This is all well and good but—"

Olivia's eyes grew wide and she stood a little taller. Avaline glanced over her shoulder, following the woman's gaze.

A man entered the restaurant with a boy and a girl in tow. The Scott family. Their son seemed in better spirits than during the drill.

They locked eyes with Avaline and walked right up to the table.

Avaline suppressed a groan.

"Hello, Ronald." Daniel smiled at them. "Hi, Austen, and—sorry, what was your name?" He looked at the daughter.

"Elsie."

"I wanted to thank you both for your help last night," Ronald said. "I don't know how I would've coped without you."

"Glad we could help," Avaline said.

Olivia stood, extended her hand to Ronald, and introduced herself. "I've been very much wanting to meet you. How are you coping with everything?"

"Well, it's pretty hard actually. This one can be quite a handful." He ruffled Austen's hair. "It's ... it's just hard. I'm not even sure how I'm supposed to be feeling. I'm not mourning my wife, because she isn't dead. The doctor can't tell me when she'll wake. It might be tomorrow. It might be years from now. Until then, I'm just stuck in this limbo. I'm trying to hold it together but..."

"If you ever need anything, please contact me," Olivia said.

"How come you two have different types of skin?" Austen asked, pointing to Daniel and Avaline.

"Austen!" Elsie jabbed her brother with her elbow. "You don't ask things like that."

"No, it's okay," Daniel said. "My ancestors came from Africa. That's why I have dark skin. My wife's ancestors came from Europe, so she has fair skin."

Austen nodded slowly.

"Why don't we all get a big table and get to know each other better?" Olivia clapped her hands together.

Ronald nodded. "That might be nice, don't you think, kids?"

Avaline's palms grew sweaty. She glared at Daniel, her eyes pleading with him.

"Actually, Olivia," Daniel said. "Av and I were hoping for a quiet meal together. We're technically on our honeymoon."

"Oh, congratulations," Olivia said. "Say no more. We'll leave you in peace."

She replaced her chair and moved away, Ronald and his children in tow.

Avaline let out a long breath. "Lucky save, Mister."

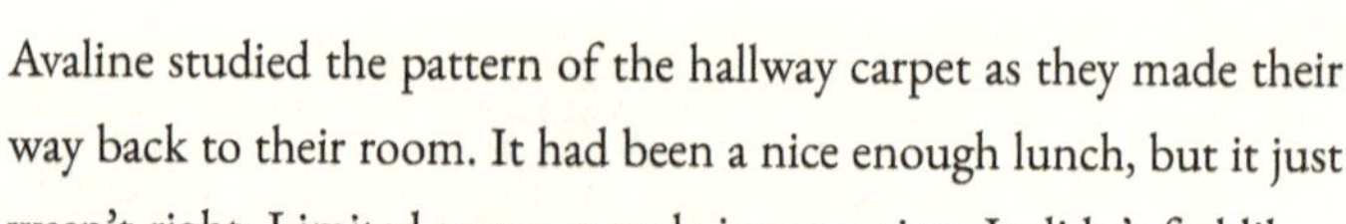

Avaline studied the pattern of the hallway carpet as they made their way back to their room. It had been a nice enough lunch, but it just wasn't right. Limited menu, people interrupting. It didn't feel like a honeymoon was supposed to feel.

"Wait up, Av. You're going too fast."

Avaline slowed, allowing Daniel to catch up.

"You know, I feel kinda guilty. Maybe we should have just had lunch with them all."

"No. There are boundaries, Daniel. We're on our honeymoon."

"Well, we're not really you know. Not anymore."

Avaline stopped. "How do you figure that?" She could feel the ice encrusting her words.

"Look around, Av. The cruise is over. We're on the run now, trying to survive."

She crossed her arms. He was right of course, but still. She wasn't asking for a fairy tale life. She just wanted her honeymoon.

"The cruise isn't over. Not yet."

"But—"

"We have a few more days before the cruise was supposed to finish. Until then, you and I are on honeymoon. After that, you can call this whatever you want. End of discussion."

Daniel nodded slowly. "Okay. I guess that makes sense, but Olivia didn't know. You can't blame her."

"I don't. I just ... I wanted this to be perfect."

"It's a bit late for perfect." Daniel chuckled, but it faded when she didn't return his smile. "Come on. Let's go do something fun."

They started walking again. Avaline gritted her teeth. A few days. Yes, she would do whatever it took to ensure that the rest of this week would be about fun, not survival.

Five

Maya knocked on the captain's door.

"Come in."

She entered.

Captain Miller was engrossed in a display only he could see. He waved her toward the guest seat next to his desk. She sat.

Miller's sanctuary looked more like a museum than an office. Model ships lined the bookshelf behind him. Sailing ships, ocean cruisers, early spacecraft. The only thing that didn't have a nautical history theme was the framed photo of his late wife.

"The looting is getting bad, Captain," Maya said. "We lost both food and medical supplies. People are panicking that we'll run out."

Miller looked up. "We have to convince them otherwise."

"If we can build up our supplies, we may be able to regain the people's trust. They'll be less likely to steal and stockpile if they believe we can provide."

"I agree." Miller swiped his finger to dismiss whatever he'd been working on, and folded his hands in front of him on the desk.

"Sir, I know you already gave your answer, but given the circumstances, I thought perhaps—"

"Maya, you're not going back into Earth space."

She nodded slowly.

"You won't have to."

She did a double take. "Captain?"

"Take a look at this." He swiped left, and a display appeared before her. "What do you make of this?"

Maya pinch-zoomed into a sensor image of a planet.

"Planet in the habitable zone of a blue giant. Early indications suggest Earth-Analogue." She glanced at the metadata. "We passed this system yesterday."

"Not exactly passed. Our course didn't take us near this world, but it is closer to Earth space than our current position." Miller swiped his finger again. "This is what we picked up on active scan this morning."

It was a faint transmission. The waveform was familiar. She played the audio.

"A distress signal?"

"A human distress signal."

"What's it doing out here? We don't have any colonies this far from home."

"That's the big mystery, isn't it?"

"Captain, we have to check this out."

Miller raised a hand. "I know. But we've also detected some alien activity in the general area. That's one of the reasons we didn't head toward this planet in the first place."

Maya studied the readings. "No alien ships in the system, Captain. They're several star systems away."

"Which is why I'm authorising your original idea of a shuttle mission. I'm not willing to take *Jewel of the Stars* that close to the enemy. Go and investigate the planet. If it's a secret Earth colony, then they'll have supplies. We'll wait for you at this rendezvous point."

A mark appeared on her display.

"What if there are people who need rescuing?" she asked.

"If it's anything like our other colonies, the aliens will have killed everyone. But if there are survivors, we'll have to rethink things."

"Thank you, Captain. I didn't expect you to agree so easily."

Miller shrugged. "We're at a stage where this type of risk is justified. But I'm sure I needn't remind you what a significant loss you or Braxton would be to this ship. I expect you to come home alive."

Maya smiled. "We will, sir."

"Good. If, for some reason, we are unable to meet you at the rendezvous location, we'll transmit new coordinates through a coded channel at 0600 tomorrow morning."

"You've thought this through."

"I've given a lot of thought to a lot of things, Maya. I need to become more than a cruise captain. I've done a lot of reading. Which brings me to a secondary objective."

"A secondary objective?"

"Most colonies have a local cache of a portion of the stellarmesh. I imagine this would be especially important for a secret base. The colony computer probably contains a great chunk of recorded human knowledge. I'd like you to bring back as much data as you can."

"Do you have any particular data in mind?"

"We need knowledge if we're going to survive, but as a society of people, we also need literature, music, film. The more we can beef up our entertainment library, the easier it will be to keep people happy and engaged."

"Bread and circuses, huh?"

Miller gave her a knowing look. "Humans haven't changed much since Roman times, have we?"

"You can count on us, Captain."

Jaylen pressed the door chime. Moments later, the door slid open. A thin woman with a pretty face wearing a flimsy floral dress stared back at him with raised eyebrows.

"Brigitte Dubois?"

"Yes, that's me."

"You're the sous chef for the main dining room?"

She nodded. "What's this about?"

"I'm Jaylen Banks, ship's Security Chief. May I come in and speak with you?"

"It's about this morning, right?" She stepped back and motioned him inside.

Jaylen made his way into Brigitte's cabin. The drab metal walls were decorated with pictures of landscapes.

He took a seat in one of the chairs. It was surprisingly comfortable for a stall cabin. Brigitte sat on the bed and crossed her legs. He tapped his wristband, instructing it to record the conversation. Was he staring at her legs? He glanced up to her face.

"Tell me about your encounter with the intruders this morning."

"There's not a lot to say. I was at work early, tidying the kitchen. I couldn't sleep. Especially after that drill." Her accent was lyrical, almost melodic.

"I can understand that. A lot of us are having trouble sleeping, lately. What time was this?"

"About four. I usually start at five for breakfast."

"So you were in the kitchen?"

She nodded.

"Where were the intruders?"

"In the secondary food store."

"And that's adjacent to the kitchen?"

"Oui."

"Is there another way in?"

"No, just the one."

"So they'd have had to go past you to get in?"

"They must have." She shrugged. "I had my head deep in the pots cupboard. An elephant could have strolled through without me knowing, so long as it was quiet."

"What finally drew your attention?"

"They weren't quiet. They knocked over a stack of tins."

"Is that when you went in?"

"I wanted to know what the noise was. I found four of them. All men."

"You're sure about that? Didn't they have their faces covered?"

"You don't need to see the face to tell the difference." She pushed her chest out a little.

"I suppose so. You're quite observant. What else did you notice? Weight, height?"

"It was hard to tell. They were bent over, stuffing food into their pillowcases. One of them was a head taller than me. I noticed as he fled. That would make him close to," she glanced upward. "Two metres."

"Did any of them speak?"

"Only as they left. The tall one. He said, 'The Crimson Guard are in charge now.'"

"Accent?" The Crimson Guard? What was that?

"North American."

"Can you be more specific?"

"Not southern. That's all I can say."

"What about skin colour? You must have seen hands, maybe arms."

"Three were white. But one of them was black, a slightly lighter shade than yourself. He was the one who spoke, the tall one."

Jaylen nodded. "Did they leave as soon as they saw you?"

"Essentially. I stood in the doorway and yelled at them. I had a frypan in my hand. They grabbed their pillowcases and ran."

"So they all went right past you, into the kitchen?"

"Oui."

Jaylen stood. "Thank you for your time, ma'am. If you think of any details, please contact me."

Brigitte stood. "You can count on it."

Jaylen let himself out. He leaned back against the bulkhead and closed his eyes. Two teams hit different locations on the ship at the same time. One mentioned a name—the crimson guard. Different speakers each time. The pillowcases could have been a coincidence, but this? What if they said something similar to Nurse Ranford? Would she be recovered enough to remember more details?

It looked like they were facing more than just random looters. This was beginning to look like organised crime.

Six

Maya checked her pistol for the fourth time since leaving *Jewel of the Stars*. Her clammy hands stumbled over the slick metal. She squirmed in the copilot's seat, next to Sue Drark, the pilot.

"Nervous, Staff Captain?" Sue asked.

"I'm fine." Maya glanced over her shoulder.

Braxton sat quietly, staring at his boots. Alexa Books, their security officer, sat next to him. They were both strapped into their seats, as the shuttle had no artificial gravity. She stared into space like a zombie. Alexa swiped her finger in the air every now and then. Reading with her eye lenses. Alexa gave a little chuckle. Must be a comedy.

"If I could have your attention?" Maya asked.

Alexa blinked and sat up straighter, looking Maya in the eye. Braxton also turned to face her.

"Once Sue lands the shuttle in the settlement, our first objective is to locate a food source. Alexa and Sue will load as much as they can into the cargo bay.

"Braxton, see if you can locate a police or military facility. We could use more terrestrial ammunition. All we have at the moment is what you brought back from the *USS Boston*."

"And that won't last long if we encounter another of those aliens," Braxton said. "We already know space rounds are useless against their exoskeletons."

"Are we expecting to encounter any hostiles?" Sue asked.

"No," Maya said. "We've been monitoring alien movements. They've been slowly picking off our ships and colonies. They were at this planet three days ago, so in theory they've moved on."

"Best to be cautious though," Braxton said.

"I still can't believe there's a colony this far out that we never knew about," Sue said.

"Doesn't surprise me," Braxton said.

"If the aliens have already been and gone, what makes you think there'd be anything left to find?" Alexa asked. "Won't they have blown the colony to pieces?"

"Our scans show the colony is still there. The aliens tend to kill the people but not destroy their surroundings." Maya shifted in her seat. "They'll blow up ships, but even on the *Boston*, they boarded and fought the crew hand-to-hand."

"That brings us to something uncomfortable." Braxton cleared his throat. "There'll probably be bodies. Lots of them. Maya and I have been in combat before, so we've seen death. How do you two think you'll handle it?"

Alexa shrugged. "I work security. I've seen a body before."

"A single body is one thing," Braxton said. "A whole lot of bodies is another. Just saying."

Maya turned to the pilot. "What about you, Sue?"

She hesitated. "Honestly, I don't know."

"Just remember," Maya said. "No matter how hard this gets, we're doing it for our people. To keep them alive. To give them hope."

Sue nodded. "Approaching the planet. I'm taking us out of warp."

Maya braced herself for the slight shift. The shuttle quaked. That was rough.

Maya turned to look out the cockpit. The planet hung below them, bright blue oceans and rich orange landmasses. Strings of cloud clung to the surface like frosting on a cupcake.

A spacecraft screamed past them, almost colliding with the shuttle.

"Whoa!" Sue grabbed the control stick and banked to starboard.

The unknown ship's main hull was smaller than their shuttle, but spider-like appendages stuck out in all directions, giving it a greater size overall.

The unknown ship banked one way then another, flying an evasive pattern.

A bright bolt of energy flew from behind the shuttle straight for the spider ship. There was an almighty flash. One of the appendages broke off.

"Who's attacking them?" Braxton asked.

Maya glanced over her shoulder as Braxton shrugged out of his harness and floated toward the front of the cockpit.

Maya brought up a rear view on her monitor. Her veins froze solid. A rectangular brick of a ship bore down behind them. It was only a quarter the size of the alien vessel they'd fought during their escape from Earth space, but clearly built by the same beings.

"What are they still doing here?" Sue asked. "Long range scans showed no ships in this system."

"Never mind the why," Maya said. "Get us out of here, Sue!"

"I'm trying."

The ship shook.

"Shrapnel from that spider arm," Sue shouted. "It impacted our warp ring."

"Damage?"

"Uh, yeah."

Sue's fingers flew over the controls as she manoeuvred them out of the line of fire of the two alien vessels.

"Gonna try to get us out." She mashed her hand on the launch control. Nothing happened. "Stars!". Sue slammed her fist into the bulkhead. "Ring is offline. I can't take us to warp."

"Then get us away from the battle," Maya said.

Sue powered the thrusters, and the shuttle shot forward. Maya stared at her console, following the movement of the two ships.

"See if you can get us around the other side of the planet," Maya said. "The more distance between us and the battle, the better."

The shuttle shook violently, like they'd hit a brick wall. Maya's harness dug into her shoulders. Alarms blared. She winced at the sound.

"They're shooting at us now." Alexa dragged her hand through her hair.

Maya turned to Sue. She stared back in a daze, blood trickling from her temple. "Sue, are you okay?"

Sue just stared back. Her mouth hung open.

"I'm taking over helm controls," Maya said. She switched control to her console and swiped her finger across the steering pad. Another bolt of energy flew toward them. Maya pulled left to evade, and the blast sailed past them, grazing their deflector.

If only the shuttle was armed so they could shoot back. The alien ship fired at the spider ship, then again at the shuttle.

Maya banked to port. *Crash!* They'd been hit again. More alarms.

Maya checked her instruments. "We're losing altitude and going down too steep," she said. "Engines are sputtering. If I can't even us out, we'll burn up in the atmosphere."

Maya's fingers raced across the console like a concert pianist. There was so much to keep track of all at once. Diverting power from the warp ring might help.

Crash! They were hit again.

"We're entering the atmosphere. One way or another we're going down."

"Can you put us down safely?" Braxton breathed on her neck.

"I don't know. I haven't flown a shuttle in years, and we're pretty banged up."

Maya clutched the console. Every part of the ship was shaking. Ice ran up her spine and into her chest. They broke through the upper atmosphere. Green ocean filled their view.

"There's land that way." Braxton pointed.

"I'm trying to aim us there with descent thrusters."

Maya's body began to press down into her seat as the planet's gravitational pull made itself known.

"It's working," Braxton said.

The land grew closer and closer.

"This is gonna be rough," Maya said. "Hold on tight"

Braxton helped secure Sue, then moved towards the rear of the cabin.

"We're coming down too fast." Maya redirected all available energy into the descent thrusters.

She could make out trees now. They were seconds from impact.

The beach! She aimed the shuttle for the sand. It might break their fall a little. The descent thrusters strained. Maya's heartbeat thrashed in her ears.

"Impact in three, two, one."

Maya's entire body shook and her spine almost ripped itself out of her back. The ship bounced back up and bunny-hopped along the beach. *Crash. Crash. Crash.* Pain shuddered through her.

With the creaking of metal, the ship came to a stop.

Seven

Pain. Maya's legs were at an odd angle. She stretched out. Good, they worked just fine. A dull ache throbbed across her head.

She blinked a few times and tried to sit up. It didn't make the headache any worse. She surveyed the cabin of the shuttle. Alexa was stirring. Sue was looking around the cabin, wide-eyed, and Braxton was missing.

Maya stood.

"How bad is it, Commander?" Alexa rubbed her neck.

Maya dropped back into the copilot's chair and brought up a diagnostic. Red warnings flashed all over the screen.

"The shuttle's been in better shape." She turned to Sue. "The question is, how's her pilot?"

"Confused." Sue rubbed her temple and winced. "We crashed?"

"Afraid so. I tried to bring her down as safely as I could. Sadly, not as well as you could have."

"I dunno. We're all alive. I'd call that a victory."

Maya turned to Alexa. "Grab me the first aid kit, would you?"

"Yes, ma'am." Alexa scurried to the back of the cabin.

Footsteps sounded at the airlock. Braxton entered.

"I'm no engineer, but the warp ring has seen better days."

Sue stood, took a step, and stumbled.

"Take it easy," Maya eased Sue back into her seat.

"Here." Alexa handed her a small box.

Maya opened it, applied an antiseptic spray to Sue's head, and pressed a sterile dressing onto the wound.

"My head is killing me," Sue said.

"We'll get you a painkiller."

"I'm so tired."

"Did you lose consciousness at all?"

"No. I was just a bit dazed."

Maya fished around for a painkiller. "I know you want to sleep, and it would probably help you heal, but we need you. Braxton or I can fly this ship, but neither of us are engineers. You are our best hope at getting this ship off the ground." She pressed a paratakamine dispenser to Sue's neck. "Give that a second, and you'll feel a lot better."

She refilled the dispenser and pressed it to her own neck. "I'll think a little clearer if I take a dose as well." It tingled against her skin.

"Okay." Maya stood and helped Sue to her feet. "Let's assess the damage. Sue, do you need help to walk?"

"I'll manage. I don't want to spend the rest of my life on this planet."

Maya took her hand anyway. "Let's take it easy to start."

They made their way to the airlock. Braxton stepped out to make way for them. They stepped down onto the orange soil of the planet.

"I think I can manage on my own," Sue said.

Maya released Sue's hand. They walked a steady circle around the shuttle. When they reached the port side Sue stopped.

"Grep!" she swore.

Sue wasn't one to use that kind of language. Her exclamation told Maya all she needed to know.

Avaline frowned out the observation window as people shuffled past behind her. Daniel rested his arm on her upper back, touching skin just above her dress.

"There are never any decent views anymore." She shook his hand away.

"We're at warp all the time."

"That's my point. When we're at warp, there's nothing to see. Would it kill them to drop into normal space occasionally, maybe next to a picturesque nebula?"

"It might."

"I guess so. Though there hasn't been any sign of alien ships since we entered unexplored space."

"That we know of. The crew could be keeping it under wraps."

"It's possible." She shrugged. "In any case, taking a walk along the upper promenade is much more fun when there's a beautiful view."

Daniel chuckled. "You don't really expect the captain to stop just for us, do you?"

"Of course not. I'm just dreaming."

"Anyway, there is a beautiful view here."

She spun back to the window. "Where?"

Nothing. The windows showed nothing but blackness.

She turned back to Daniel. His eyes were locked on hers. Oh. Her cheeks warmed.

"Well, aren't you the charmer."

Daniel leaned forward and pulled her into a kiss. She wrapped her arms around him. The ship and everyone else aboard melted away. The two of them encompassed the entire universe.

Eventually they separated.

Avaline took Daniel's hand and they strolled along the promenade.

"We need a hot date. The magic show is on tonight. Then maybe we can squeeze in a late-night swim before the pool closes. She grinned at him, but he wasn't grinning back. There wasn't a flicker of sparkle in his eyes. What was wrong?

"Actually, Av, they're holding a memorial service tonight for Maaka Henare, the security officer who died on the *Boston*."

"And you want to go?" Avaline flinched.

"Yes. I do. It's important. The guy gave his life to save us all."

Avaline's mouth dropped open. She didn't bother to close it.

"Going to some ceremony won't bring him back, Daniel."

"That's not the point." He gazed at his shoes. "They should have cancelled the magic show, now we're not really on a cruise anymore."

"Not everybody is expected to attend the memorial. It's mostly for the crew. I mean, there's no way all the passengers will fit in the hall. Besides, I've been looking forward to the magic show since we first booked this cruise."

"You're right. But I want to be there. You don't have to come if you don't want. Go watch the magic." Daniel turned. "I'll honour the dead alone," he muttered under his breath.

"Hold it. Don't walk away from me, Daniel Barrett."

He stopped and looked over his shoulder.

"That was pretty harsh. If it means that much to you, of course I'll go."

"Thanks, Av." There was no joy in his voice. "I appreciate it."

Avaline let out a long, slow breath. Everyone kept telling her the cruise was over. Who knew when they'd put on another show. She might have just missed her last chance.

Reporting to the captain always felt like a trip to the principal's office. Not that Jaylen had ever been sent to the principal's office. He'd always been a good kid.

Miller motioned Jaylen toward a plush couch. "Coffee?"

"Yes please, Captain. It's been quite a day."

"So I'm told." Miller poured two mugs from a pot in a nook next to his desk. He handed one mug to Jaylen and then sat in a plush chair opposite the couch. "Bring me up to speed."

"Well, there was the theft of food from the restaurant. That's to be expected, to a certain extent. People are afraid. They don't know how long our food stores will hold out, so they're wanting to stockpile as much as they can. But the medical supplies robbery has me concerned."

"How is the nurse holding up?

"Nurse Ranford will be fine physically. Psychologically, she's pretty shook up."

"I wish we had a counsellor on board, but it's not the kind of thing you need on a short-term cruise." Miller sipped his coffee. "Have a look through the passenger manifest. See if there is anybody on board with a background in counselling."

"That's not a bad idea, Captain." Jaylen tasted his own coffee. The warmth travelled down his throat into his belly, creating sparks in his brain almost immediately. "But I haven't told you the worst part."

Miller raised an eyebrow.

"At one incident, the perpetrators made mention of the Crimson Guard. An organisation, maybe?"

Miller leaned forward. "Are you telling me I have organised crime on my ship?"

"It's a possibility, Captain."

"Stars!"

"As you say."

"You've got to be very careful about this, Jaylen."

"What do you mean?"

"If word gets out, we could have another riot on our hands. I'm sure you don't want that."

"No, sir. But to be frank, that's not my first concern."

"As Security Chief, keeping the peace on this ship is your responsibility."

"Yes, and the best way to do that is catch the intruders."

Miller put his mug down on the coffee table. "Of course I want you to find these people, but I need you to take the secrecy aspect seriously. It is of vital importance that we not cause a panic. Otherwise the Crimson Guard will be the least of our problems."

Jaylen's fists clenched. The captain was more concerned with preventing panic than catching the culprits. The important thing here was to nip this Crimson Guard in the bud before it took root. No matter who found out about it. This was too important for discretion, but orders were orders.

"So what's your first step?"

Jaylen pulled himself out of his thoughts. "I'm going to get the housekeeping staff to assess any missing or dirty pillowcases."

Miller stared at him blankly.

"They used pillowcases as masks, and to stash their stolen goods in."

"Very well. I trust you'll come up with a suitable reason to give the housekeeping staff?"

"I'll think of something."

"Then I won't keep you from your duties."

Jaylen stood, nodded to the captain, and strode out into the hallway. He had to investigate a crime without letting on there was a crime. Brilliant. Just brilliant.

Eight

Maya dropped onto a relatively flat rock. The blue sun beat down, warming the area.

"We need to decide our next step."

"What next step?" Sue held a hand to the wound on her head. "We're stranded on an alien planet, and there are hostiles up there." She pointed to the sky. "I'd say this is game over."

"You take that attitude, and it is." Braxton took a seat on another rock.

Maya stared at the dirt. Silvery blue fronds grew among the gravel. This planet's equivalent of grass? It looked more like a succulent than a leafy plant, but the colonists here had used it as a ground cover. She looked up at Sue. "The nearest settlement is that way, right?" She pointed inland.

"Yeah. Only about a kilometre away."

"Are you certain there's no hope for the shuttle?"

"It's pretty banged up. Some of the damage can probably be fixed, but the warp ring is trash."

"Okay. You take a closer look and see what can be repaired. I want a thorough assessment of what it would take to make it fly again." Maya turned to Alexa. "You'll carry out our original mission. I want you to find whatever supplies you can and bring them here."

"Here?"

"Yes. Load it into the shuttle."

Sue snorted.

"Don't forget it's not just about food. We need data. If you can find a primary data core, we may be able to take a significant cache of the stellarmesh back to *Jewel of the Stars*. That would be very helpful. Once Sue is done with her assessment, she can help you."

"But—" Sue said.

"Braxton." Maya turned to make eye contact with him. "You will survey the area and make a threat assessment—the aliens in orbit, that spider ship, any indigenous life. I want to know it all."

"No worries." Braxton tipped his head.

"What's the point of loading supplies into a ship that won't go anywhere?" Sue asked. "It's pointless."

"That's why I'll be out there looking for alternatives. Another ship we can either cannibalise or fly away in."

"Maybe we should wait to see what you can find, and then load the supplies wherever is most appropriate," Alexa said.

"Yes," Sue said.

Maya shook her head. "The longer we spend here, the more we put ourselves at risk, and everyone back home. I want the supplies gathered here as soon as possible."

Sue slapped her legs, then stood. She paced, shaking her head.

"That's an order." Maya said.

"An order?" Sue glared. "I'm not a soldier, and neither are you. I'm pretty sure the cruise line won't be paying me a salary any longer. Why should I do what you tell me?"

"Because I'm in command of this mission, and right now you are a soldier." Maya stepped right up in Sue's face. "You will learn to follow orders, or you can remain behind on the ship in future."

Sue and Maya locked eyes. The glare continued for several seconds. The intensity in Sue's stare waned.

"Fine." She stormed off toward the shuttle.

"You have your orders, people."

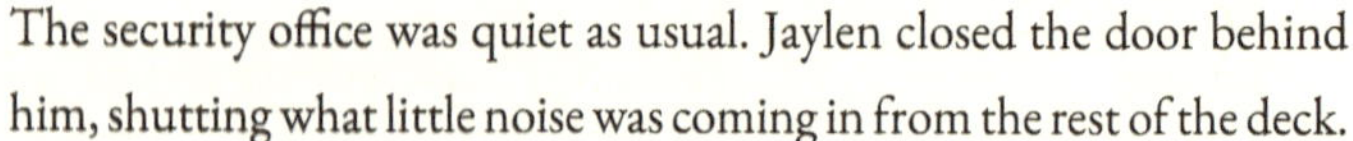

The security office was quiet as usual. Jaylen closed the door behind him, shutting what little noise was coming in from the rest of the deck.

Nari Jin, his second-in-charge, sat at the front desk.

"How'd it go with the captain?" she asked.

"He seems more concerned about preventing a panic than finding the culprits." Jaylen shrugged. "Whatever. We have a job to do." He wandered over to the coffee machine and pressed a few buttons. He was going to need a lot of cups today.

"I spoke to Bonnie Ranford, the nurse," Nari said. "Her memories are still a little sketchy, but she has confirmed a mention of the Crimson Guard."

"Well, that's it then. There's no doubt anymore. The two events are connected."

Nari gave a slow nod. "She also said he spoke with a New Zealand accent."

"She's sure? It wasn't Australian?"

"This was the point she was most clear on. Said one of her cousins married a New Zealander, so she knows the difference."

Jaylen sipped his coffee. He allowed it to sooth him. "Who's in charge of housekeeping?"

Nari pressed a few invisible controls projected by her eye lenses. "Marge Cunningham."

"Can you call her in, please?"

"Done."

He carried two steaming mugs over to the desk and handed one to Nari. "What we need are some suspects. I'd like to know who on the ship has a criminal record." He dropped into the seat beside her.

"That sounds good in theory, but we're not police officers."

"Yeah. Ordinarily I'd have to request this information from Earth-based authorities, but with the stellarmesh down and earth under alien occupation, I don't have that option."

"We'll need to work with what we have."

"Which, in terms of the passengers, isn't a lot. We have their names and some family connections."

"We should have most of their public social profiles. We cache them as a matter of course."

Jaylen nodded. "That could give us occupations." He pressed a control on his wristband, syncing a virtual screen with Nari and himself. "Collate the profile data into tabular format. We need to look for anything that might indicate a predilection for criminal behaviour."

Nari nodded.

"It's weird." Jaylen took another sip. Nice and strong. Good. "The people we generally have on board don't belong to the lower socio-economic classes that would tend toward becoming thugs and crooks. People who can afford a cruise are usually well-off middle class types."

Nari gave him one of her looks. "Being rich doesn't make a person good."

Jaylen chuckled. "Obviously, but you get what I mean, right?"

"I suppose so. Don't forget the culprits might be staff members."

Jaylen nodded slowly. "That's an unpleasant thought."

"The kind of stress we've been under this last week could push anybody to criminal behaviour."

"You're right, of course, but this is more than that. Random rioting and looting I get, but this is organised crime. I could imagine something like this forming over time, but it's too soon. Somebody must be pulling some strings." He straightened in his seat. "So what've we got on staff? There's job and income information. Performance reviews. Police checks. Add the staff details to the table."

Nari nodded slowly. "The list is ready." A large sheet of data appeared before them.

Jalen scanned down the rows. He let out a little groan. "This is gonna take forever." He turned to Nari. "You know what we need to do? Recruit some admin staff to assist us."

"Okay."

Jaylen sipped his coffee. He closed his eyes, savouring the taste, letting it work its magic. "Y'know, something's bothering me."

"Hmm?" Nari looked up.

"The Crimson Guard. Why invent a silly name for themselves, and why say it? It's like they went out of their way to ensure we knew they belonged to this group. I can't think of a good reason for them to do that."

"Intimidation? They want us to know that they're at work, so we'll fear them?"

"But to what end? No, there's something else going on here. I just wish I knew what it was." He took another sip. "This list is a good start, but we need a more solid lead."

The door opened. A middle-aged woman entered. "Marge Cunningham. You called for me?" She bit her lower lip.

"Ah, yes. Please take a seat. We have a job for you."

Nine

Avaline glanced at the time display. The memorial service must be nearly finished. They'd paid honour to Maaka Henare. They'd fired a probe loaded with flowers into space in lieu of a body. Then a crew member had chanted a karakia, in keeping with the man's Maori heritage.

In truth, it had been good to pay respects. The guy lost his life in service to all of them. It just wasn't how she'd planned to spend her honeymoon. Daniel had been quiet throughout the proceedings.

Seemed like Captain Miller was winding things up. Good. They might be able to catch the end of the show. Maybe this evening could still be salvaged.

"Now I'd like to take some time to talk about another hero to all of us. Haylee Scott."

So much for winding up.

"Mrs Scott is still with us, but is even now in a coma, fighting for her life. Our hearts go out to her husband and children. I think we should all spare a thought for them during this time."

Avaline nodded.

"Haylee's husband Ronald has asked to say a few words."

A torrent of conflicting emotions roared inside Avaline as Ronald made his way up to the front. Annoyance that she was spending her night here, instead of the main theatre. Guilt that she was annoyed. Compassion for Ronald and his family. Righteous selfishness. Everyone else got to have a proper honeymoon. Why should she be denied that?

"Thank you all for coming here this evening, to remember Maaka Henare, but also to pay honour to my wife." Ronald leaned on the podium. "It hasn't been easy for us. We have a special—needs son. Now that my wife is in a coma, I'm caring for him and his sister alone."

In the end, she'd come here tonight with Daniel, the dutiful wife, because it was the right thing to do. But why had he insisted on coming in the first place? Why was this more important to him than their honeymoon. It was like he wasn't prioritising their marriage the way she was. What did that mean for the future?

"My wife is the kindest, most loving person I have ever known." Ronald's voice trembled. "I wanted her to stay here with me, but she knew she was needed on the *Boston*. She risked everything for you, and for me. And I think we should all honour her for that."

People stood to their feet around Avaline. Daniel shot up. Avaline glanced around and rose.

"We all owe her our lives. Every single one of us. I just..." Ronald put his head down. A good twenty seconds ticked by. He raised his head again. "I just wish I could tell her how proud I am of her." His voice was choked by tears. He sniffed and gave a nervous laugh. "For some reason, I thought it would be a good idea to come up here and talk. Not sure why."

Captain Miller joined Ronald at the podium and put his arm around the man. "Let's all take a moment of silence to be grateful for Haylee. I'd invite you all, in the privacy of your own minds, to hope and pray for her full recovery."

Avaline closed her eyes and thought of Haylee.

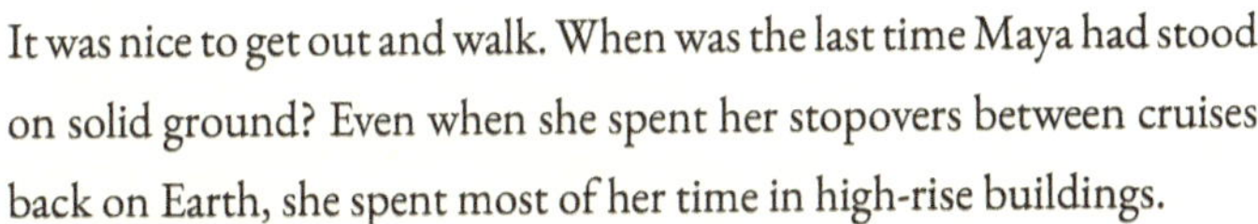

It was nice to get out and walk. When was the last time Maya had stood on solid ground? Even when she spent her stopovers between cruises back on Earth, she spent most of her time in high-rise buildings.

The sky on this planet was a familiar blue, but beyond that, the planet was distinctly alien. That's what it was. Maya hadn't seen a hint of green since arriving here. She took in the trees nearby. Orange leaves. She looked to the ground. The rubbery blue succulent spread as far as the eye could see. The effect on the pale blue hill was breathtaking.

Maya puffed a little as she climbed the hill. She'd be putting in more time in the crew gym when they got back. Still, the top of this hill would be a fantastic vantage point to survey the area. If there was another way off this planet, this was where she would find it.

A strange mewing drew her attention. A herd of animals grazed down on the plain below. Their bodies were vaguely cow-like, though rounder and they had humps on their backs, longish necks, and snouts that resembled anteaters. Maya smiled. What would their meat taste like? No doubt the colonists here had made their own local steaks.

The animals stamped and sniffed the air, and their mews turned to squawks. Something was agitating them. The ground shook slightly as they stampeded into the distance, out of sight. What had spooked them?

Trees crunched as a tall lizard bounded into the clearing. It was somewhat reminiscent of a T-Rex, but it hopped like a kangaroo. Maya laughed, glad to be safely out of the way. Crystal would love it here. She'd always liked kangaroos—one of the reasons she'd wanted to stay in Australia with her father. Maya sniffed. Who was she kidding?

Crystal had stayed in Australia with her father because she couldn't stand to be in the same room as Maya. Her daughter was lost, and there was probably no way to get her back.

Maya reached the crest of the hill. She drew a deep breath as she took in the surroundings. Blue-grey ground and orange trees stretched out as far as she could see. There were no other townships in view. It seemed the main colony was the only outpost on this part of the planet.

Wait.

What was that, in front of the trees in the distance?

Maya drew out the compact binoculars she'd pilfered from the emergency survival pack in the shuttle. She zoomed in on a metallic grey box shape. It was well camouflaged on this planet, but it was definitely a ship. The ship that had attacked them.

The aliens must have been so busy with the spider ship that they hadn't noticed where Maya's shuttle had crashed. With it's systems offline, there wasn't much for the aliens to detect on sensors. Tall four-armed creatures milled around their ship. Didn't look like their ship had any damage. They were here to hunt.

Hunt for humans.

Jaylen looked down at the list of names. It was short, but not as short as he liked.

"What do you think?" He turned to Nari.

"It's all theoretical at this point. Any of these people could be involved in the Crimson Guard, or none of them. These are just the people our algorithm has suggested might have a predilection for criminal behaviour."

"Actually, we know that many of them have priors because it's a matter of public record on the social network." Jaylen stood and wandered over to a blank wall. He projected a screen over it.

"Let's look at our suspects," he said. "First of all, in the restaurant, we have a group of white males, lead by an African American male, two metres tall."

"There are only two African Americans here," Nari ran her finger down the list.

"Put a star next to both of them."

"Done."

"Next, the raid on sickbay was done by a man with a New Zealand accent. Do we know skin colour?"

"I checked with Nurse Ranford," Nari said. Light skin this time. We don't have a height, though."

"Actually, I think we do. Bring up the security footage."

Nari pressed a few invisible controls. A new screen sprang into existence in the middle of the room.

Jaylen watched with Nari as the pillow-cased man rummaged through the drawers. The door to Haylee Scott's room opened. Nurse Ranford appeared. Ranford's eyes and mouth went wide. The thug stood.

"Pause."

The image halted, the look of terror frozen on Ranford's face.

"Look there." Jaylen pointed to the thug. "He's standing up straight at this point. See how the top of his head matches the lights embedded in the wall? The bottom of those lights are exactly 1.6 metres from the ground."

"How do you know where his head stops under that pillowcase?"

"The pillowcase is pulled down hard. See here? You can make out the curve of his head."

"You're right."

Jaylen waved, dismissing the screen. "The guy has quite a bit of strength behind him He's not huge, but he did some damage to Nurse Ranford."

Nari winced.

Jaylen walked back to the front desk. "Let's see where that leaves our list." He scrolled through and added a couple of stars.

"I think we have a list of suspects."

"Seven names."

"You take the New Zealanders. I'll take the Americans."

Ten

MAYA REACHED THE PAVEMENT of the road in the main settlement, stopped, doubled over, and took great gasps of air. She'd run the whole way back.

Braxton was just a block away, walking toward her. She took a moment longer to catch her breath before she started, slowly this time, in his direction.

They could use some kind of communication device for missions like that. They had communicators back on *Jewel of The Stars*, of course, but they all ran off the ship's wireless network. Maybe Sarah could modify their wristbands to communicate with each other, in a peer-to-peer fashion. It would sure save some running.

"You're in quite a hurry." Braxton crossed his arms and leaned back his heels, a stupid grin plastered on his face.

"It's the aliens."

"The ones who shot at us from orbit?"

Maya nodded. "And they look like the same species you encountered on the *Boston*. Four arms. Long snouts."

"Yep. That's the ones. The same occupying Earth."

"We need a name for them. Something other than 'the aliens'."

A grin cross Braxton's face. "I can think of a few choice descriptors."

Maya frowned at him. "Not helpful."

"Not good news, anyway."

"You're a gifted understater, Commander. Not only do we have to find a way off this rock, but we have to avoid alien attack while doing so. Do you have anything to report?"

"I do, actually." He pointed his thumb over his shoulder. "Back thataway. Spotted the spider ship. Was just about to go check it out. Maybe it's salvageable. We could fly it outta here."

"I dunno, Braxton. That ship has a massive target painted on it. The aliens will shoot it down on sight."

"What do you suggest?"

"We could try taking their ship."

"That's a major military undertaking. Much easier to slip off in the spider."

"Well let's check it out first. It's moot if it's in no condition to fly."

Braxton motioned with his arm. "After you."

***

Avaline held Daniel's hand as they walked the corridors.

The magic show would be over by now.

"Want to go for a swim?" She stroked his fingers.

"Not really. Not now."

"Well, let's at least grab a drink or something."

"To be honest, I'd rather just go back to our quarters, Av. I don't feel like partying, not after that."

Avaline let go of his hand and walked the rest of the way in silence.

They reached the door. Daniel swiped his hand and it opened. He held his hand out for Avaline to enter ahead of him. She strode in and stopped in front of the porthole.

They were at warp, so there was nothing to see through the round window. No starscape, just a blotch of white light surrounded by black.

"Are you going to talk to me, Av?" Daniel stood behind her. His reflection glared from the window.

Avaline crossed her arms and turned. "What is there to say? You're obviously not interested in having a honeymoon with me anymore." She took a small step closer.

"Of course I am." Daniel paced the room. "It was one night. That service was important. And you agreed to go with me."

"This isn't just about tonight."

"You really think everything that's happened on this ship is my fault? That I'm somehow plotting to ruin your precious honeymoon?"

Avaline bit her lip. "My honeymoon. That's the root of the problem, isn't it?"

"What is this really about?"

"You seem to go out of your way to let circumstances rob us of our right. I'm here fighting, clinging on with my fingernails to this honeymoon so it doesn't slip out of our grasp. But you're not fighting with me, Daniel. You obviously don't want it like I do. That makes me wonder if you want me at all."

"Stars, Av! I want you." He almost spat the words. "I love you, but you're not making this easy. Of course I wanted a honeymoon. I wouldn't have used my savings to bring you on this cruise if I didn't. I'm trying to make the best of what's happening, but I'm not gonna bury my head in the sand. The honeymoon we dreamed of is over. It's gone, and it isn't coming back. We have to accept that and move on. Make the most of what we've got."

Avaline wiped a tear from her cheek. "So there it is. You admit it. You've given up trying."

Daniel's face softened. He took a step toward her and reached for her hand.

She considered a moment, then let him take it.

"Why is this so important to you? Why are you acting like this? You're not a self-centred person. I know you, but this?" He waved his free hand up and down in her direction. "I don't know this."

Avaline sniffed. "Yes. I'm being self-centred. Don't you think I know that? I have a right to be. A honeymoon is the one time in a person's life when they're allowed to be selfish."

"And you think if we don't have a proper honeymoon now, you'll have missed that chance."

Avaline nodded.

Daniel scratched his chin. "When did selfishness become something you aspired to?"

Avaline opened her mouth a crack.

"Have a nice night. I'll find somewhere else to bunk down." Daniel turned and strode up to the door. It slid open. He took one more step and was gone. The doors slid shut with finality.

When did selfishness become something you aspired to?

"Daniel?"

It was too late. He was gone.

Tears formed in her eyes.

Jaylen sat in the quarters of Tyrell Armstrong. He'd covered the basics—work history, previous record. Tyrell frowned and crossed his arms.

"Man, enough 'bout my past, okay? I got some history. We all do, but that's way behind me."

"Certainly. I understand you used to work for Summins Holdings. They're a New Zealand company, right?"

"Yeah."

"You ever been to New Zealand?"

"Once or twice. Not recently. What's this all about?"

"Just investigating some events last night, Mr Armstrong."

"And you think I had something to do with this? Because I got a record?"

"We're not targeting you Mr. Armstrong. We have a list of people"

"Yeah? Well, I had nothing to do with anything."

"One last question. Can you tell me your whereabouts last night at 4:30 AM?"

"I was in bed."

"Can anybody corroborate that?"

Tyrell shook his head. "Nah. I'm afraid I didn't share my bed with anyone last night. Wasn't for lack of trying." He shrugged. "What's a brother to do?"

Jaylen nodded. "I understand." He stood. "I think that will be all for now. Thank you for your time."

Tyrell stood. "You don't think I did it, do you?"

"My investigation is in its early stages at the moment, Mr Armstrong. I'll let you know if I need anything further from you."

"Yeah, all right." Tyrell walked him to the door. Jaylen exited, and let the door slide shut behind him. This guy was hard to figure out. He certainly had the means, a big tough guy like that. He was the type of man who could sway people, attract a crowd. He had a history of violence—An incident involving a woman, years ago. He'd spoken openly about it on his social profile. Then there was the matter of his trip to New Zealand. It was a tenuous possible link to the intruder in sickbay.

Jaylen strolled down the hallway. It would be interesting to see how Nari was getting on with her interviews.

A door sounded behind him. Footsteps approached. The hair on the back of Jaylen's neck stood on end. He turned. Two large men, pillowcases covering their faces, bore down on him.

Jaylen raised his hands in anticipation of an attack. It came from both of them at once. Two fists knocked his hands out of the way and pummelled his face.

Jaylen fell backward against the bulkhead. He steadied himself with his right hand.

Blood rushed through Jaylen's veins. He leapt back up and pulled his fist back for a punch, but they struck again before he had a chance. One punch to the gut doubled him over, then another on the chin thrust him back again.

Jaylen collapsed to the floor, gasping for breath.

A foot collided with his gut.

Jaylen knew nothing but pain.

"Lay off your investigation." A harsh voice whispered in his ear. "The Crimson Guard are here to stay. You've been warned."

Jaylen gasped for air and turned, willing his eyes to focus on the retreating blurs.

Maya gagged as she neared the crashed spider ship. Smoke. Her eyes stung. The vessel had come down right on top of an industrial warehouse. Debris lay scattered around the ship. It was hard to tell what was building and what was spaceship.

"Okay, let's take a look." She shielded her eyes.

"Wish we had Sarah with us."

"I dunno." Maya surveyed the wreckage. "Don't think even Sarah could do much with this thing. It's pretty bad."

The metallic protrusions that made the ship look like a spider were bent, misshapen, and burned.

Maya waved her arm, trying to disperse some of the black smoke emanating from the wreck.

"This looks like a hatch." Braxton grabbed a broom and wedged the hatch open.

Inside was a small compartment. Controls lined the interior walls. A small cushion covered in harnesses sat in the centre.

"What sort of creature would fit into a space like that?" Maya scratched her head.

"I dunno, but whatever it was, it must be resilient. The impact from a crash like this would have killed a human."

"Maybe they have more advanced inertia control than we do."

"Maybe." Braxton shrugged. "Either way, it seems something survived. It's probably close."

"You think it's hostile?"

"Our favourite aliens were shooting it for a reason."

"They didn't seem to have a reason for invading Earth."

Braxton shook his head. "Oh, they had a reason. We just don't know what it was." He drew his pistol. "We don't have a lot of ammo. Let's hope this alien doesn't have thick skin like the invaders."

Maya drew her own pistol.

"There." Braxton whispered, pointing. "In the shadows." He pointed to Maya, motioned toward a tall pile of metal containers, then pointed to himself and indicated the other side.

Maya nodded and crept toward the containers. She held her pistol out in front, finger hovering near the trigger guard.

One foot after another. She slinked to the edge. Taking a deep breath, she raised her weapon and spun around the corner.

Nothing.

She crept past the container. This side of the warehouse was something of a maze. Piles of containers blocked direct line of sight to the other end, where Braxton was advancing.

Maya strode up to the nearest pile and spun around.

A noise like the squeal of an angry pig pained her ears. Something large, bulbous, and white vanished around the corner.

Maya ran in pursuit, ready to fire. Around the corner, a white six-legged shape crawled clumsily toward Braxton. He let off a warning shot. Sparks lit up just in front of the creature. It turned. They had it cornered.

The creature squealed again and cringed against the interior wall of the warehouse.

Maya stepped close, gun aimed at the creature's head.

It was stocky and round, about a metre in diameter. It didn't stand erect, instead crawling along on all six. The skin was white and flabby. Wide human-like eyes stared back at them, above a circular mouth.

"Well, what do we have here?" Braxton asked.

Eleven

MAYA LOWERED HER GUN and holstered it. Braxton still had his weapon trained on the creature.

An alien. A real living alien. Being shot at by alien spacecraft was one thing, but to see an extra-terrestrial being in the flesh, to stare into its eyes, that was another.

"Do you think it's intelligent?"

"Hard to say. Doesn't look it, but something was flying that spider ship." He turned to the creature. "How about it, mate? That ship back there yours?"

"You don't honestly expect it to answer, do you? Not like it's gonna speak English."

"I guess so. Well, we have a couple of options. Kill it, lock it up, leave it here, do nothing."

"We can't justify killing it. He's clearly more afraid of us than we are of him. He's not a threat."

"He?"

Maya shrugged. "Looks like a he." A spot of red blood was seeping down one of the alien's limbs. "He's hurt."

She crept forward and kneeled down. "I'm not going to hurt you," she said in as soft and non-threatening a voice as she could manage.

She took hold of the limb. The alien flinched a little but didn't pull away. She pulled out the first aid kit from the shuttle and rummaged around for an antiseptic spray. "This might hurt a little."

"You sure you wanna do that?" Braxton tipped his head.

"You want him to get infected?"

"You don't know his physiology. Is he allergic to that spray?"

Maya bit her lip. "Give me your water."

Braxton used one hand to release and toss his canteen to her, while keeping his sidearm trained on the alien with his other hand. "Use it sparingly."

Maya unscrewed the lip and poured a little water on the alien's wound. He flinched.

"Braxton, help me. I need a dressing." Braxton didn't move. "I don't think you need to keep the pistol trained on him."

Braxton lowered his weapon. Slowly. He grabbed a dressing and handed it to her. She wrapped it around the limb. "Clasp?" Braxton handed one to her.

"There you go." She fastened the dressing in place. "All good as new."

"We should lock it up. It might tell the others about us."

"He's clearly not the same species that you described meeting on the *Boston*, and our enemies were attacking him."

"They could have had their reasons. Maybe he's bad. Could be worse than them."

"I dunno." Maya stood and dusted her hands off. "Enemy of my enemy and all that."

"I help." The creature spoke in a raspy but strong voice.

Braxton raised an eyebrow.

Maya turned to the creature. "What?"

"I help." It pointed at Maya.

"You help ... us?"

"How can you speak English?" Braxton asked.

The alien held its left front forearm to its ear. The limb sported a hand with an opposable thumb.

"You listen?" Maya asked. "You can learn English from hearing us speak?"

"I Nilf. Nilf learn."

"You're saying your species has an innate ability to learn languages?"

"Learn."

She turned to Braxton. "We should take him with us."

Braxton frowned. "I dunno, Maya."

"We have a common enemy, and he's offered to help us. He obviously belongs to an advanced species, technologically, they're at least at the same level as us. Think of what we could learn from him."

Deep furrows formed in Braxton's forehead. "You're the boss."

Jaylen reached out to steady himself as he stumbled through the door into sickbay. The ship was spinning around him.

"Jaylen?" A warm Jamaican accent. He looked up into Doctor Clarke's wide eyes. "What happened to you?"

"What's it look like? I got beat up."

"Up here, now."

Clarke reached out two strong arms and helped Jaylen onto the examination bed.

She poked and prodded him in several places. Each time he winced and groaned as the pain in that area intensified.

"I need to see if you have any cracked ribs."

She waved a device over his torso, poker—faced the entire time. A slight trilling sounded from the device.

"How did this happen?"

"It's part of an ongoing investigation. I think I'm getting too close."

"Would you like me to inform Nari?"

"That'd be great."

Clarke put the device down.

"So?"

"You're lucky. A lot of bruising, but nothing is broken."

"Then pump me up with something for the pain, and I'll be on my way."

"Not so fast. You need some rest. I'm not sending you out there to chase crooks in this condition."

"This is important, Doc."

"So are you. This is not negotiable. You'll rest, and you won't leave this sick bay until I say so."

Jaylen frowned, but it turned into another wince as the pain grabbed him somewhere in his left side.

"Don't worry. I'm not gonna keep you in here forever, but you need to take care of yourself a bit."

It was hard to deny how tired he was. Nightmares every night. Then the evacuation drill, followed by the early morning theft report. How long had it been since he'd had a full night's sleep?

Jaylen lay his head back and closed his eyes as Doctor Clarke pressed something against his neck.

The world grew quieter, dimmer, as the pain began to fade.

Maya let out a contented sigh. Base camp was a surprisingly beautiful sight. Sue and Alexa both sat on stones next to the shuttle.

"What's all this then?" Braxton called out in a jovial voice. "Sitting down on the job. What a pack of bludgers."

Sue glared at him. Alexa gestured with her middle finger while smiling. "While you've been out sightseeing, we've lugged a cargo bay full of supplies from all over this city."

"Yeah, yeah." Braxton grinned.

Sue and Alexa's faces dropped as the Nilf scampered into view. It was comical—even cute—the way it walked on all six legs. It was surprisingly quick, given how fat it was.

"Stars! What's that?" Sue asked.

"This is Nilf," Maya said.

"Yintol," Nilf said.

"Pardon?"

It stopped and pointed to itself. "Yintol."

"Not Nilf?"

"Species Nilf. Name Yintol."

"It speaks English?" Alexa stared at Yintol, wide-eyed.

"A little."

Alexa stood and circled Yintol.

"We've been chatting with him while we walked. It's amazing how much he's picked up. Every sentence we say, he learns several new words. His ability to contextualise them is incredible."

"Where'd he come from?"

"Yintol was the pilot of the spider ship." Braxton dropped onto a rock.

"Can't say much for his grammar," Sue said.

"He seems to be concentrating on vocabulary for the moment," Maya said.

"He can really figure out the meaning of words just from the context?"

"That's what we're guessing." Maya peered into the shuttle's cargo bay. "Looks like you've done well with the salvage." She turned to Sue. "Status report on the ship."

"A lot of the damage is repairable. It won't be pretty, but I can get us back into orbit if you're not too worried about meeting safety standards."

"Sounds good."

"Don't celebrate yet. Like I said earlier, the warp ring is the real problem. I'm not even talking about the buckling, though that's a significant problem. I had a look inside, and the plasma coils are fused. Completely useless." She tossed a burned—out component onto the ground in front of Maya. "Without them, we can't establish a warp bubble around the ship." She shrugged. "We're going nowhere."

Maya scratched her chin. They'd come this far. She was not letting a fused plasma coil defeat them.

"What if we could find new coils in the settlement?"

"Already tried that," Alexa said. "Found a military bunker. No plasma coils. We did get plenty of guns and ammo."

Braxton grinned at this.

"What about the aliens?" Braxton asked. "Could we steal one of theirs?"

Sue shrugged. "No doubt their ships use something similar but it won't help."

"Why not?" Maya crossed her arms.

"I'm not an engineer. I can patch up some minor damage, but replacing the plasma coils? You'd need the chief engineer for that."

"The chief engineer isn't here." Maya glared at Sue.

"You see my dilemma."

Maya stepped forward, right up in Sue's face. "Listen to me. If we don't get that ship fixed we'll be stranded on this planet forever. Is that what you want?"

"Doesn't matter how mad you get at me, Maya. I can't become an engineer, anymore than you can spontaneously transform into a brain surgeon." She raised her arms above her head an then let them drop back against her thighs. "Even if I had the knowledge, how do you know the alien coils would be compatible with our technology?"

"I help," Yintol said. Everyone turned to him. "We steal. I help fix. I know."

"You can get the coils installed?"

"I know coils. I can fix."

Maya looked at Braxton. He shrugged. "Okay. Looks like we have a plan."

"I don't trust him." Braxton crossed his arms.

"Neither do I, but we're stranded on this planet. If he can help…"

"We need to keep a close eye on him."

"Agreed."

"All right. But let's get some rest first," Braxton said. "It'll be dark soon, and we've been at it since leaving the ship. It'd be morning there by now."

Maya nodded. "We start at first light."

Twelve

Avaline rolled over. The lights were fading up. Must be morning. She reached out for Daniel. Her fingers found only sheets. Where was he?

Oh. Yeah. They'd had a tremendous row last night. He'd left the cabin. Avaline had been up half the night and had eventually cried herself to sleep.

Surely he'd have come home. He couldn't have stayed out all night. Perhaps he was in the bathroom?

Avaline climbed out of bed, still in yesterday's clothes. She popped her head into the en suite. Nothing.

A torrent welled up inside her chest. He really was mad at her.

He'd given her a lot to think about. She'd taken this honeymoon thing so much to heart that she'd put selfishness on a pedestal. In her mind, her selfish attitude was a virtue. She shook her head at her foolishness.

But staying out all night? Daniel had overreacted. She balled her fists.

But this was no time to be mad at him. They needed to reconcile their differences, not play blame games. She'd shower, put on clean clothes, and search the ship until she found him.

She scratched at her wristband. So irritating. Wait. She didn't need to search the ship. She could just consult the computer to locate his wristband.

She pressed a control. "Locate Daniel Barrett."

The band beeped. *"Pattern not found."*

Great. He must have turned off location tagging. Okay. Back to the original plan.

The lights flickered, giving the hallways of the *USS Boston* a creepy quality. Jaylen clutched the pistol in his hand. Before him, the monstrous creature hissed, its back to him.

Jaylen emptied his clip into the creature. It didn't even turn.

Ahead of it, Maaka floated, shooting his own sidearm. To his right, Haylee Scott screamed.

The alien advanced.

"Get out of there," Jaylen shouted, but they couldn't hear him. "Run!"

He pressed the button to fire his suit's thrusters, but he moved further away, rather than closer.

The alien lunged.

"No!" Jaylen screamed as the alien skewered Maaka with its pronged appendage. It turned to Haylee.

"Get out of there, Haylee!"

It was no use. His mouth was moving, but no sound came out.

The alien plunged its other talon into Haylee. Blood burst from her chest, floating about like little red marbles.

Tears streamed down Jaylen's face. Why couldn't he have saved them?

The alien turned.

There was death in its eyes. No. This wasn't right.

It lunged at Jaylen.

He tried to fire, but his empty pistol clicked.

The alien raised its forearm and thrust its claw into Jaylen's chest.

Jaylen opened his eyes. His pulse boomed through his wrists and temples. Not again. How many more times would he have the nightmare?

He took a long slow breath to calm himself.

Jaylen surveyed sickbay. A nurse he didn't recognise was on duty. Ranford would be recovering for a while, and not just from her physical wounds. The pain he'd seen behind her eyes would not go away quickly.

Jaylen understood that. He'd recently faced his own beating.

"You've had a bit of a rough night, Mr Banks," Dr Clarke said.

"Yeah. Somebody mistook me for a punching bag." He rubbed his neck. "So tell it to me straight, Doc. Am I gonna live?"

Clarke smiled. "You'll live, all right. You're tougher than you look."

The door slid open and Nari strolled in. "How are you feeling, sir?"

"Like a Rigellian swamp moose trampled on my back."

"Did you get a look at them?"

"'Fraid not."

"Pillowcases?"

"Yep. I must be getting close. They feel threatened, so they attacked me to warn me off."

"I suppose that's a good sign." Nari took a seat next to his bed. "Speaking of pillowcases, Marge Cunningham reported back. A bag of 50 pillowcases has gone missing from linen stores."

"Which means we're not going to nab anyone by the mysterious absence of pillowcases from their stateroom."

"Did any of your attackers speak?"

Jaylen looked up at the ceiling. "One of them whispered in my ear. He didn't say much—but I'm sure it was a New Zealand accent. How'd you go with your interviews?"

"Not a lot of luck. One was in a wheelchair, one was clearly too short, another was too tall, and one was Maori. That just leaves one suspect, Aiden Harris. I haven't managed to locate him."

"This ship is finite. He can't hide forever."

Nari nodded. "What about you? You said you were getting close. Do you have a suspect?"

"The last guy I spoke to. Tyrell Armstrong. He's got a short temper and a history of violence. And no alibi."

"He the only one?"

"There was one other man without an alibi, Michael Sline, but he doesn't strike me as the type. Armstrong made a big point of saying he spent the night alone, but not for want of trying. Given the number of female conquests plastered all over his social profile, it seems strange that he'd have had no luck."

"He's reasonably attractive."

"And he has something of a charismatic personality. I think he wasn't with a woman because he was busy planning a robbery."

"But how do we prove it?"

"A line-up would be good. The sous chef is a witness, but she didn't see their faces. She did hear his voice, though." He closed his eyes. How to deal with this. "We could bring him in for an interview and have the sous chef listen in from outside. Then she can tell us if it was his voice."

"I don't know if that would hold up in court, but it could be worth a try."

"For a court, we'll need a judge. I wonder if there's one on board." He sat up a little straighter. "Ultimately, that's the captain's problem. Our job is to identify those responsible.

"Want me to bring Armstrong in?"

"Soon as the doc lets me outta here."

⸺◦⸺

Maya settled into her thermal sleeping bag. They'd found ten of them in the shuttle's standard issue emergency survival pack. Alexa and Sue were already settled into theirs.

Braxton sat on a nearby rock, sidearm in hand.

"Looks like you've decided to keep watch, Commander."

Braxton nodded. His eyes didn't leave Yintol.

"Wake me when you're ready to be relieved, okay?"

Braxton said nothing, just continued to stare at Yintol, who was rolling up into a ball. A large ball.

"Yintol, where are you from?" Braxton asked.

The alien said nothing.

"From. You." Braxton pointed, but the alien wasn't looking.

"Etera."

"And where is that?"

"Far. Very far."

"Why were the aliens attacking you?"

No answer.

"Why aliens attack you?"

"Attack many."

"What were you doing in this system?"

Yintol emitted a sound that was part snore and part purr.

"Well, all right. You sleep." Braxton crossed his arms. "My questions will still be here in the morning."

Maya chuckled and rolled over to face Alexa.

"What was the colony like? Have you learned anything about it?"

"It was interesting. Not a lot of housing, but lots of scientific and engineering facilities. Seems the only people who lived here were working on something. No evidence of families."

"And the..." Maya swallowed. "The bodies?"

"We saw them." Alexa's voice went quiet. "All adults."

"So this was a secret research facility."

"Seems that way. My guess is they were working on something illegal, or at least commercially confidential, which is why they were out here in unexplored space. We grabbed a bunch of data drives. Maybe Sarah McLaughlan can decipher some of it. But there was one thing. A logo. Seemed to be a common theme. It was an orange star with a blue oval behind it."

"Marsden Engineering," Maya said. "So we've got a secret facility jointly run by an engineering company and the military. Makes sense. Marsden contracted with the space navy a few years back." What had they been up to? "When we get back to the ship, we can go over the information you've recovered and see what it was all about."

"Interesting," Braxton said. "If I'm not mistaken, Marsden is a Dalia Spring company."

Maya rolled back toward him. "You know she's on board the *Jewel*, right?"

"Yes. I know." Braxton nodded slowly.

"Half the companies on Earth are owned by Spring."

"Bit of an exaggeration, but yeah. Although that doesn't prove anything."

"Anything about what?"

Braxton shrugged. "Nothing. Doesn't matter."

Maya sighed and got into a comfortable position. She wasn't going to get anything more out of Braxton tonight.

❖

Avaline walked down the corridor toward the observation lounge. She'd explored the buffet and the gym. He'd probably spent much of the night in a bar, but he wouldn't still be there now. Not at this hour.

The observation lounge was filled with bench seats. A huge floor-to-ceiling window curved the entire circle of the room. Beyond the window lie the star-studded vista of space. They'd dropped out of warp. Good. It'd been too long.

She stood a moment, taking in the view. If only Daniel was here to share it with her. She began a search pattern, flicking her glance across the lounge to the end, then back again along the next row.

Daniel was here, at the end of the next row. She quickened her pace. How would he respond to her? Would he push her away? Be angry? Glad to see her?

Her pace slowed as she neared his seat. She bit her lip. "Daniel?"

He turned. He looked like grep. His hair was a mess, his face contorted, and his gaze unfocused. He smelled of lager. "Av?"

"Yeah."

She eased down into the chair next to him.

"My head hurts."

"Seems you had quite a night."

"Uh. Yeah. Uh, Av, look, I'm sorry, I ..."

"It's okay. I'm sorry too. You need some water. Let me get you some." She stood and made her way over to the water cooler. After filling a cup, she took it back to his seat and handed it to him.

"Thanks, love." He sipped the water. "Guess I had a few too many last night."

"Seems so."

"About what I said to you—"

"You were right. About the whole selfishness thing. It was stupid of me."

Daniel took a swig of water and coughed.

"You right?"

Daniel nodded. "Thing is, Av, I don't want you to think I'm not into this honeymoon, I mean, I wanted a magical time just as much as you did. I've been grieving the loss of what we could have had ever since the captain announced the invasion."

Avaline smiled. "Why was that memorial service so important to you?"

"My grandfather. He died in the Pacific War. I barely got to know him. Every Remembrance Day we'd honour him. My grandmother, dad, and uncles would all tell stories about him. I know so many. I guess it just became an important part of my life to honour the sacrifice of those whose lives were taken in defence of others. When I heard about Maaka Henare, it all came flooding back. His family back on Earth won't know of his death. They won't know to honour him. So I felt a responsibility to do it on their behalf."

"That's beautiful, Daniel. Why didn't you tell me this earlier?"

"What can I say? I'm a bloke. We don't talk about this stuff." He took another sip of water. "But I'm glad I did now. This is what marriage is meant to be all about, right?"

"Exactly."

"What's say he have a special night of it tonight?. We'll take some food back to our cabin, have our own little private picnic. Then, after that, maybe we can have a little fun." He grinned.

Avaline tipped her head back. "Nice idea, but you're rubbish at planning romantic stuff. Why don't I do the organising. I'll get everything set. Let me treat you. Then after dinner, you can treat me."

They leaned in to kiss.

"Ooh, you stink." Avaline pulled back. "Go take a shower and make yourself human while I start making plans."

Daniel gave a little mock salute. "Aye aye, captain."

Thirteen

Jaylen motioned Tyrell Armstrong into the seat in the tiny interview room. Jaylen had never needed to use this space before today.

He glanced over his shoulder. Brigitte Dubois, the sous chef, would now be standing on the other side of the one-way glass. Nari had been keeping her hidden away in the locker room.

Jaylen tapped his wristband, bringing up the controls for the interview room. He swiped an icon which piped the audio out into the viewing area so Brigitte could hear. He then pressed the record button and sat.

"This is a recorded interview conducted by Security Chief Jaylen Banks, with Mr Tyrell Armstrong in the security office of *Jewel of The Stars*, on the twelfth of March, 2294."

Tyrell Armstrong glared at Jaylen, arms crossed. The man had come here reluctantly and was clearly not in the mood to be involved in such proceedings.

"Mr Armstrong. I understand you spent some time working in New Zealand."

"Yeah. I told you that last night."

"I understand that, but this is now on record, so we might need to repeat ourselves a little."

Armstrong rolled his eyes.

"Can you tell me about the business associates you met while in New Zealand?"

"Man, I don't remember. It was years ago. What's this got to do with anything happening here and now? What's this even about?"

"Please bear with me. There may be a connection."

"There ain't no connection with me 'cause I ain't involved."

Jaylen leaned forward. "Humour me."

"I don't remember. I think there was a girl named Lucy. Nice legs. Don't remember nobody else."

"Perhaps this will help." Jaylen swiped a photo of Aiden Harris toward Tyrell so it would display in his eye lenses. "Do you know this man?"

Tyrell's eyes widened a fraction. He stared down at the table. "Never seen him before."

"That was a quick answer. Are you sure you don't want to take a closer look?"

"I tell you I don't know him."

"Okay. Does the name Aiden Harris mean anything to you?"

"No, it doesn't." Tyrell leaned across the table, his nostrils flaring and his eyes wide.

"Calm down, Mr Armstrong. No need to get aggressive. I'm just asking a few questions."

Tyrell thrust a finger in Jaylen's direction. "I think you got it in for me. I don't know why, but you think I had something to do with this Harris. But I don't know Harris, and I ain't involved in any crime, so unless you got some evidence, I think we're done here."

Jaylen nodded. In truth, Tyrell had told him all he needed to know.

"Thank you for helping us with our enquiries." Jaylen stood and opened the door. Tyrell was halfway out before Jaylen could even motion toward the exit.

Jaylen stepped out, took a quick glance at the black curtain which hid Nari and Brigitte, and escorted Tyrell into the corridor. Tyrell left without a word of goodbye.

Jaylen grinned and returned to the office. Nari was already pulling the curtain back.

Jaylen locked eyes with Brigitte. "So, Miss Dubois, what do you think? Was that the intruder's voice?"

"Ah, I dunno." Her left hand fidgeted with the edge of her dress, just below her cleavage.

"What do you mean, you don't know?" Jaylen crossed his arms.

"Well, it was hard to tell, you know. It might have been him. Maybe it wasn't."

Jaylen maintained eye contact, doing his best to ignore the woman's obvious attempt to draw attention down to her chest.

"Well you must have some idea. Did it sound similar to the man's voice or not?"

"I only heard a few words during the break-in, and I was nervous. I'm sorry. I wish I could be more helpful."

"All right. You can go, Miss Dubois. We'll let you know if we need anything further."

Brigitte scampered out of the security office. Jaylen turned to Nari.

"That was odd. You think fear of the moment may have caused her to forget his voice?"

"More likely the opposite. When being threatened, the voice of the assailant tends to get burned into a victim's memory."

"Something's going on with her. What's she trying to hide?"

Les Miller's wristband beeped and a notification appeared at the lower-right of his field of vision.

Appointment: Dalia Spring

Wonderful. The last thing he needed this morning was a rich business tycoon sticking her nose into the running of his ship. He'd let her have her say, then dismiss her as quick as he could.

The door chimed. Les swiped an icon to open the door and stood.

For such a powerful person, Dalia Spring was a surprisingly diminutive woman. She only came up to Les's shoulders. She was flanked by a man and a woman, both a head taller than Les.

Dalia dismissed them with a wave. The door slid behind her, shutting them out.

Les extended his hand. "What can I do for you, Ms Spring?"

Dalia descended into the chair opposite the desk.

"I see this as more of an introductory meeting, Captain. It is my intention to establish a dialogue with you regarding various matters of life on board this ship."

"Indeed." Les crossed his arms.

"Yes. I'm interested in a number of issues—food distribution, shipboard services—but perhaps the most critical issue of the day is the ship's destination."

"Well, Ms Spring, we don't have a destination at the moment."

"And yet we've been travelling at warp almost constantly since leaving known space. We must have been going somewhere."

"Somewhere, yes, but not anywhere specific. We're in uncharted space. You could say we're exploring."

Spring frowned. "I don't think many people on board signed on to be explorers, Captain. Frankly, I'm surprised. I'd have thought you'd have a more considered system in regard to setting your course."

"It's been pretty much a case of putting as much distance as possible between us and Earth, in hopes of evading the aliens. So far, so good." Les shifted under Spring's unfaltering gaze. "When I'm satisfied we're out of immediate danger, we'll chart this region of space, looking for the best potential sources for food and other raw materials."

Spring nodded. "I'd appreciate being informed when the time comes to begin making those assessments, Captain."

"Ms Spring." Les at up straighter. "I don't think there's any need to bother you with these matters. I can assure you that the crew of this ship is well qualified to take care of any need that may arise. My advice to you is to sit back and enjoy the ride. There will likely come times when all people aboard the ship will need to contribute something to the ongoing survival of our community. I'm sure we'll find something suitable to your unique set of skills. In the meantime, let us handle things."

"Captain Miller, you seen to be under the mistaken impression that I'm asking you for a favour. I am not. I expect to have a voice in matters of shipboard policy."

"You may be one of the richest people on Earth, but we're not on Earth, and you have no more authority on this ship than any other passenger."

Spring stood. "I'm afraid you're misinformed again, Captain. You see, when we left Earth, I was in the process of finalising my purchase of United Earth Cruise Lines. I booked this trip because I wanted to travel on one of the ships I was about to own. That means, Captain, that I am your employer, and the single highest authority on this vessel."

Les clenched his jaw and rose. "You can't possibly be serious."

"I can see you need some time to digest this information. I'll let you ponder this new arrangement and check back in with you later." She turned and stepped toward the door. It slid open.

"Good day, Captain Miller."

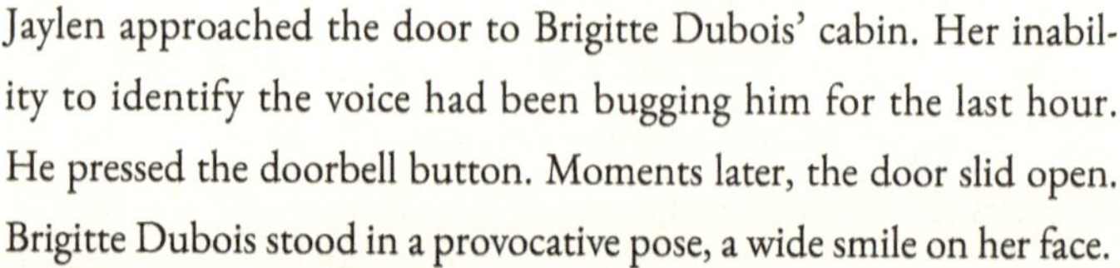

Jaylen approached the door to Brigitte Dubois' cabin. Her inability to identify the voice had been bugging him for the last hour. He pressed the doorbell button. Moments later, the door slid open. Brigitte Dubois stood in a provocative pose, a wide smile on her face.

At the sight of Jaylen her smile dropped into a deep frown. "You again? What do you want now?"

"Expecting someone else?"

"That's none of your business." Brigitte walked into her cabin.

"True." Jaylen followed her in. "I wanted to go over your reaction to the interview again."

"I told you all I could."

"You didn't tell me anything. You were noncommittal. Calculatedly so."

"I wasn't sure."

"I don't believe you. The intruder threatened you. His voice is seared into your memory. The man I interviewed today is either the same man, or he's not. Which is it?"

Brigitte crossed her arms over her chest.

"I can stand here all day if necessary, Miss Dubois."

"It wasn't him. Not the same man."

"You're sure of that?"

"Positive. Happy?"

Jaylen looked Brigitte up and down for a moment. "Very well. Thank you for your time."

Jaylen showed himself out of Brigitte's quarters. He tapped his wristband, and swiped Nari's name from his list of contacts.

"Jin here."

"Nari, it's time to do a little surveillance on our favourite sous chef. I want you to place a notification on Brigitte Dubois' door. Let me know as soon as she leaves her cabin."

"Understood."

Fourteen

JAYLEN STRODE DOWN THE hallway. A little map was displayed in the top-left corner of his field of vision. Brigitte Dubois, represented on the map by a red dot, had left her quarters a few minutes ago.

Brigitte was headed toward the stern of the ship. The only area of interest on deck 7 aft was the botanical garden. Dubois had no reason to be in the passenger areas of the ship. She wasn't on duty, and her job involved very little passenger contact.

Jaylen rounded the corner just as Brigitte pushed through the double doors into the garden.

Jaylen took a discreet seat on a bench near the door.

A communication notification appeared in the top-right of Jaylen's view. He swiped the notification to the centre.

"Jaylen, it's Nari." The voice came from his wristband.

"What's up?"

"Tyrell Armstrong is on the move. He's headed your way."

"How far away?"

"About twenty metres."

"Thanks."

Jaylen stood, turned, and pretended to busy himself with a wall panel.

An attachment appeared next to Nari's notification. Jaylen dragged it onto the map. A blue dot appeared. Tyrell.

The blue dot continued to move until it was right next to Jaylen at the door of the garden. Jaylen turned in time to see Tyrell's back pass through the door.

"Bet you anything they know each other."

"Seems possible," Nari said.

"Meet you in the office."

Jaylen sprinted to the nearest lift and caught it to the security office. Nari was waiting for him at the front desk when he entered.

"According to the map, they've interacted a little. They're currently both near the pond."

"Thanks, Nari." Jaylen flopped into the seat at his desk and accessed the security footage from the camera closest to Brigitte's cabin. He scrubbed through time, looking for any evidence that Tyrell Armstrong had been there. Nothing.

Well, that wasn't surprising. Passengers weren't allowed on the crew decks. He switched to a camera near Armstrong's cabin. It was a little further away than the previous shot, but he scrubbed through, looking closely.

He went back one day, two, three, four. Then she appeared. Brigitte Dubois was standing outside Tyrell Armstrong's quarters. She pressed the chime and waited a moment. The door opened, and she entered. Jaylen glanced at the time index. 23:00. Seemed Tyrell's bed hadn't always been empty.

Jaylen rolled back in his chair and clapped his hands. "Gotcha."

The walk back to Avaline's stateroom was becoming a hike thanks to the baskets she carried in each hand, loaded with goodies for their special night. She stepped over to the wall of the corridor and placed her baskets on the ground. She stretched her arms and rubbed her biceps. Too much time in the library these last years, and not enough time in the gym. That was gonna change. This ship had a nice gym. She'd have to put some hours in.

She scratched her wrist. Stupid wristband. Why society insisted everybody wear them was beyond her. Surely there was a better way to interact with the stellarmesh. Maybe a chip in the head or something.

She removed the band and tossed it into one of the baskets. It settled in somewhere between the fresh bread and the bottle of wine. She'd spent several days' dinner rations on these supplies. It didn't matter. They could rough it once they reached the official end date of the cruise and their honeymoon was officially over. Her expectations for anything after that time were considerably lower.

Tonight was going to be special. She'd see to that. She picked up the baskets, swapping hands. The food basket was much heavier than the other, which contained cut flowers from the garden on the promenade. It didn't seem as though anybody had seen her take them, but surely they wouldn't begrudge a girl a few flowers on her honeymoon.

She walked towards her cabin. *Their* cabin. Avaline and Daniel had maintained separate dwellings through their engagement. Sharing ownership of a home, even if it was just a cabin on a cruise ship, was new and exhilarating. Avaline would have had it no other way.

Footsteps sounded behind her. Several people. They were coming up close. Avaline glanced over her shoulder. Two faces scowled back at her.

Avaline drew in a sharp breath and quickened her pace. Blood raced through her veins. What did they want?

As she turned to face forward again, her foot connected with the edge of a room service trolley.

Her heart clenched as she tumbled forward. She let go of the baskets as she threw her hands out in front to cushion her fall.

Ouch. A shockwave reverberated through her body.

The wine!

She glanced up, through the pain, to see where the baskets had landed. There, to the left. No sign of broken glass or spilled wine. That was all that mattered.

As she struggled to her feet, one of the men behind her picked up the baskets.

Avaline winced as she stood to full height. She reached out her hand for the basket. Rather than hand it to her, the man turned and jogged back the way he'd come. With her food. And wine. And flowers.

"Hey!" she yelled.

She ran after the guy and tried to wrestle the basket from his hands.

The other man was now in front of her.

"Relax, lady," the man said. A Kiwi? "All we want is the food."

"In your dreams." She kicked the man in the shins. He grimaced. "That's mine."

A hand grabbed her by the collar.

"Cool it, lady."

She was lifted from the ground. Her heart clenched. With a push she was thrust through the air. Crash. She hit the bulkhead and collapsed to the floor.

Avaline shook herself and looked up as the two men disappeared around the corner.

She made a fist. She'd never catch them now.

She reached for her wristband to report the theft. The wristband wasn't there.

That's right. She'd left it in the basket.

She opened her mouth to swear, and then stopped. The wristband. They had it. The computer could track it for her.

But then what? Could she really hold her own against those two guys? She was fit and knew some self-defence, but it was two against one.

Then again, by the time security got involved her stuff would be gone. They were probably eating it now.

Avaline stood. She'd find them.

◆O◆

Maya sat up. How long had it been since she'd slept out in the elements, on the ground? Too long. She was out of practice. Every part of her body ached.

At least the sleeping bags had been warm.

She glanced up at the sky. The blue sun was already spreading its rays across the alien landscape. She glanced at the time. They'd only slept six hours. This planet had a much shorter day/night cycle than Earth. That was probably something she should have looked up before coming here.

She stood and stretched each muscle group in turn. First her back, then her arms, legs, and chest.

Yintol slept soundly. He looked like a giant pork roast from this angle. All those fat rolls must keep him nice and warm. Perhaps he came from a cold planet. Etera, he'd said.

"Morning, Maya." Braxton rose from his rock.

"You never did wake me."

"I was fine." Braxton scratched his face. "Though I could use a shave. Should have had one before I left *Jewel of The Stars*.

"We're going to need some breakfast. We want our wits about us for today's mission."

"There's plenty of supplies in the shuttle." Braxton shrugged.

Maya stepped into the cargo bay and rummaged through the stocks. They needed something that could be consumed easily, without the need for preparation. Much as she'd hated them in the day, a military ration pack would be perfect.

She found several tins of fruit with easy-open lids and gave one each to Sue and Alexa. There should be enough sugar and fibre in the fruit to keep everyone going. She tossed one to Braxton, who stood over Yintol.

"What's your people's history with the aliens that attacked us? Where do they come from?"

"Give the guy a break, Braxton." Maya opened her tin and tipped some fruit pieces into her mouth, making sure as not to pour syrup all over herself. "He's not fluent in English yet. There'll be plenty of time for interrogations later." She looked around for a stick as she chewed. Finding one, she picked it up and searched for some sandy ground.

"We know next to nothing about this alien," Braxton said. "I'm not willing to give him a pass. I think you're being too trusting."

"Maybe. But right now, our objective is to get off this planet. He's made no attempt to hurt us. Even if he does, we're armed. I think we can handle him and figure the rest out later."

Braxton raised his hands above his head and then slapped them against his thighs. "You're the boss."

Maya used the stick to draw a crude map of the alien camp.

"There are hills here." She indicated right. "I saw guards here and here."

"They may rotate the guards around different locations." Braxton leaned over the map as he chewed his own fruit.

"Your experience on the *USS Boston* suggests these beings are extremely resilient, so I think we can agree our aim is to avoid being seen rather than trying to engage them."

"That'll be difficult, but yes. I gave that alien a bullet to the brain, and it still came back and attacked our team." He shrugged. "Must've had a backup brain, or something."

"Where would you make our approach?"

"I'd come from here." Braxton grabbed the stick and indicated the hills to the left of Maya's rough map. "We'll have cover from the forest most of the way, and these shrubs might give us a little cover as we approach."

"Maybe we should have done this at night."

"I doubt darkness would have given us any advantage. When I was on the *Boston*, the alien messed with my head. It put images in my mind to induce paranoia."

"Telepathy?" Maya stiffened her posture.

"That's my guess. I got the impression it could sense my presence as I moved through the ship. It knew where to go to cut me off. Watch out for scary stuff in your head, and the smell of cinnamon. It seems to coincide with their telepathic activity."

"So we not only need to avoid being spotted but scanned as well?"

"We need a diversion. The more aliens we can lure away from their ship the better."

"But if there's even one left ..."

"We're guessing here, Maya. We don't know enough about their capabilities. How their telepathy works. But we can incapacitate a single guard, at least temporarily."

"We need Sue to explain what the plasma coil looks like, and where to find it."

"I'll see to that. And about the diversion. I'll set off an explosive charge here." He pointed with the stick. "That should draw a few of them away from their ship."

Maya nodded. It was a plan.

Fifteen

Avaline entered the promenade. She'd need to buy a new wristband and sync it to her eye lenses if she were to track and locate her old one. Now, where could she buy such a thing? She couldn't even call up the ship's directory without her band.

She walked up one side, glancing at each shop in turn. Jewellery, souvenirs, hair salon.

There had to be a security office somewhere around here. Daniel's voice sounded in her mind. "Just report it. Don't take matters into your own hands. It's dangerous. It's reckless." If he'd been here to say those things, he'd be right, of course. But even as she understood that, she knew she'd ignore it. Reckless it may be, but reckless was kind of her thing.

Wait. There, on the other side of the promenade. Technology and Communications. That would do. She crossed the promenade and entered the shop.

Her stomach twisted up like a corkscrew. This was a bad idea. No, she'd made her decision. She'd at least find out where the thieves were. If they ate her stuff, the evidence would be gone, but she could make a strong case if she could catch them taking someone else's stuff.

"Can I help you?"

A middle-aged South American man approached her.

"Yes, please. I need a new wristband."

Maya gripped the automatic rifle tightly. It fit her hands like an old friend. So much of the training from her military days came back the moment she picked it up.

She crouched behind a large bush. All around her, trees reached to the sky, their leaves a blend of pale blue and orange.

The alien ship sat in the clearing, a plain metal box, similar in appearance to a cargo container. The box was ringed with a rectangular projection resting against the hull. Their equivalent of a warp ring? How it even managed to fly in a planetary atmosphere was a mystery. She could see four guards from her location.

"If Sue is right, the lump that edges the ship should be full of plasma coils. We only need one."

Alexa held up a cutting torch they'd found in the settlement. "Just let me at it."

Boom. The ground trembled below their feet. Three aliens spun their heads to the east, stared silently for a moment, then bounded off onto the plains. They used one set of arms as pseudo-legs, galloping on four limbs at incredible speed.

Maya drew a sharp breath. That left one alien on this side of the ship. Was there another on the other side?

"I'll circle around and try to draw the alien to the other side." Maya said. "You get straight up there and cut out the plasma coil."

Alexa nodded.

Maya grabbed something that looked vaguely like a pine cone from the ground and crept low to the ground as far west as she could get without leaving the cover of the forest. She could just see around the front of the ship from here.

She pulled her arm back and launched the pine cone with as much force as she could. It clanged off the roof of the northern edge of the ship and bounced onto the ground, stirring up the gravel as it went.

The response was immediate. The alien guard brandished the claws on his upper set of arms and walked around the ship. The moment he cleared the front of the ship, Alexa was out. She sprinted over and lit the blowtorch.

As far as first steps went, the plan was going okay so far. But the guard would quickly return when he found nothing on the other side of the ship.

Maya sprinted to the front of the ship and peered around. Sure enough, there had been a guard on the north side as well. The two aliens looked towards the hills. The scent of cinnamon tickled Maya's nose.

One of the aliens spun around in Maya's direction. She pulled back. Had it spotted her? Didn't much matter either way. They'd opened their telepathic senses. They'd know she was here. And they probably knew what she was planning.

Ice flooded her veins. Her palms became so slick she could barely hold her rifle. She'd been in combat before. This was not natural fear.

This was the aliens.

"You're gonna have company," Maya shouted.

She spun around, rifle outstretched, and fired several rounds. The alien was ready. It leapt up, claws raised, catching only a bullet or two in its muscled legs.

Maya retreated backward, firing all along. The creature screamed again.

Maya chanced a glance to the right. Alexa was in a firefight with the second alien, her cutting torch abandoned on the gravel

"Fall back," Maya shouted.

Alexa grabbed the torch and retreated into the forest.

Maya turned and followed, running for all she was worth.

She sprinted past tree after tree. The aliens could move faster than humans. They'd catch up in seconds. It was inevitable. Maya was going to die.

She ran on, adrenaline fuelling her.

Death didn't come.

She ran another step. Then another. Maya glanced over her shoulder. The alien had turned back.

She continued running. She ran for another two minutes before succumbing to fatigue. She stopped, spun around and aimed her gun.

She drew in great gulps of air. Her heart pounded through her torso.

No sign of aliens.

She looked around for Alexa. There, about ten metres away. Maya joined her companion.

"They mustn't have wanted to leave their post," Maya said between breaths. "They're supposed to guard the ship, not chase us through the forest.

"Makes sense." Alexa nodded. "We could have been a diversion for another attacking party."

"Once the other aliens realise Braxton's explosion was the diversion, they'll be combing this forest. I don't think we can return this way."

Alexa nodded.

They'd failed.

Avaline crept through the narrow corridor. She shouldn't even have been able to get into this section of the ship. The "Staff Only" signs were clearly displayed in physical metal next to the door, but it hadn't been locked. No doubt the thieves had circumvented the security locks—another crime they could be charged with. Avaline couldn't be held accountable for circumventing the locks, but she could be charged with trespassing.

Her gut twisted. What if they attacked her? What if she never came back? Daniel wouldn't even know where she'd gone. But she couldn't tell him. He'd only talk her out of it.

Avaline tapped her wristband. "Dictate email for delivery to Daniel Barrett in one hour." The band beeped. "Daniel, a couple of thieves stole our food basket, and I'm going to get it back. Don't worry. I'll probably have it before you even get this message. I'm on deck ..." She looked about for a sign but found none. "Seventeen, I think." She tapped the band again.

"Message held for delivery in one hour," the computer voice said.

She turned her attention back to her surroundings. This hallway ended at a door. Her eye lenses indicated there was a large open space behind it, and her original wristband was inside.

She peered through a little window in the door. There was a catwalk above the space. That was her way in. Much better than storming through the door.

She looked around for an access ladder. There it was.

Avaline smiled. The blood was rushing through her veins like a tempest. How long had it been since she'd had an adventure? Back in her university days, they'd occasionally break into the teacher's private bar and steal wine, simply for the challenge of it. Such things were shameful, of course, for a law student, but Avaline had always hidden a little dark side. She stifled a grin at the memory.

She climbed the ladder. The metal was cool in her hands. Good thing she was wearing jeans, and not one of the skimpy skirts she'd brought on this trip for Daniel's benefit.

She climbed into a passage that was little more than a steel tube, and made her way along on her hands and knees. There was a hatch at the end which she pulled open, slowly and quietly.

The open space was right in front of her. It looked nothing like the rest of the ship. Exposed pipes ran all over the walls and ceiling.

She crawled out onto the catwalk. There was room to stand erect now, but crawling seemed less conspicuous.

Reaching the end of the catwalk, she peered over the edge. There was her basket, next to a small pile of pillowcases. A man with dark skin was taking food items out of a pillowcase and putting them into a metal cabinet.

"Hey!" A voice yelled out. Male. "Up there!"

They'd spotted her.

Avaline turned around, no longer bothering to crawl. She dropped down onto her knees when she reached the tube and shuffled through, as quickly as she could then slid down the ladder, not bothering with the steps.

The door at the end of the hallway opened. One of the thugs who'd stolen her basket ran into her.

Avaline screamed.

Rough hands covered her eyes and mouth. She struggled but couldn't break free. Another set of arms enveloped her body.

No! Why had she come alone? So stupid. They had her.

She thrashed against their strong arms to no avail. She was dragged through the door.

Sixteen

Jaylen sat opposite Brigitte in the small interview room and tapped his wristband.

"This is a recorded interview with Brigitte Dubois, conducted by Security Chief Jaylen Banks in the security office of *Jewel of The Stars*, on the twelfth of March, 2294."

Brigitte scowled at him, her arms crossed tightly across her chest. There was no longer a hint of seduction in the woman's appearance.

"Miss Dubois. How long have you known Tyrell Armstrong?"

"I don't know him."

"I know that's a lie. We have security footage of you entering his cabin at night, on several occasions during this cruise."

Brigitte bit her lip. "Okay. I admit it. We're lovers." She leaned forward, placing her hands on the table. "Making love isn't a crime on this ship, is it?"

"No, but conspiracy and theft are."

"You can't blame me for wanting to keep silent when I recognised his voice. I couldn't betray him."

Jaylen smiled and jabbed a finger in Brigitte's direction. "But I think you did more than just recognise him. I think you were in on it. I think you left the galley door unlocked so he could get in, then conveniently turned your back and engrossed yourself in reorganising the pots and pans."

Brigitte scoffed.

"So one question remains. Why'd you do it? I mean, I'm sure the … relations … were enjoyable, but they can't have been worth the risk of getting arrested?"

Brigitte crossed her arms again. "Why do you have to condemn and judge everyone? People like you are always butting your noses into someone else's business. You could use a little 'relations' yourself."

"This is my job, Miss Dubois. Do you have any idea how important the food resources on this ship are?"

"Of course I do. Everything has changed. Food will be scarce soon. I see our stores. They won't last forever. When the food does get scarce, I want to be in with those who have the food."

"And who might that be? Who else is involved?"

"I don't know."

"Come now, Miss Dubois. There's no point holding back now. You've just given me a confession. Why not share the blame? I might put in a good word with the captain on your behalf."

Brigitte shook her head. "I have nothing else to say to you."

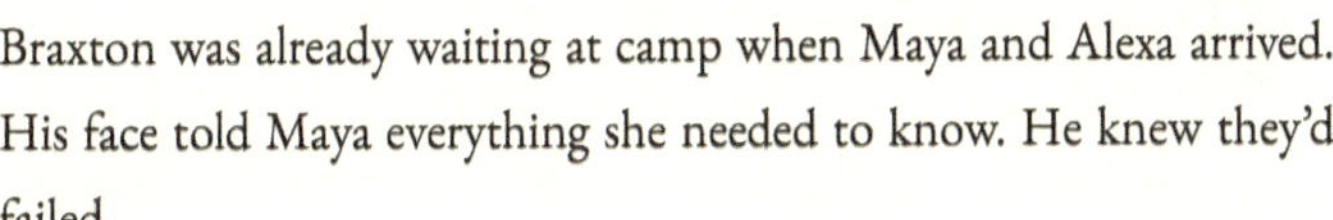

Braxton was already waiting at camp when Maya and Alexa arrived. His face told Maya everything she needed to know. He knew they'd failed.

"I'm sorry, Braxton. We were so close, but we couldn't hide from them, not with their telepathy. As soon as they suspected somebody was nearby they reached out with their minds."

Braxton nodded. "I know what that feels like."

"Maybe we should have swapped roles. You have more military experience than me."

"No, we had it right. I knew how to safely set the charges. You didn't."

"All of this is well and good," Sue said, leaning against the shuttle. "But we still don't have a plasma coil."

"We must have coil," Yintol said. "I have examined your ship. I can fix, but I must have coil."

"Then there's only one option left." Maya stood a little straighter. "Stealth is useless against telepaths. We'll have to take the coils from them by force."

Braxton gave a little tip of his head.

"Right, people," Maya said. "We go in, we attack, and we don't come back without the coils."

"Biggest problem is that there are more of them than us," Alexa said.

"And they're bloody difficult to kill," Braxton said.

"Y'know what would help that? If we can kill one and bring its body back with us, Doctor Clarke might be able to learn a little about their physiology. Figure out why they're so resilient, and how we can fight them."

"That's a good idea," Braxton said. "But it's a secondary objective at this point."

Maya nodded slowly.

"They will already have their advance scout on their way here, actively searching for us. They are probably going to be the alien's best soldiers."

"Do we have any explosives left?" Alexa asked.

"A few." Braxton gestured towards the shuttle.

"We could make mines. Take out their best soldiers before they get here."

"That might make it a little easier to reach their ship." Maya said. "Last thing we want is to fight and maybe lose the battle before we even get in sight of our objective."

"I have another idea." Sue joined the group. "You need to reach their ship, right? But they're going to make you pay a high price for every kilometre you take. What you need to do is bypass their advance guard all together."

"How do you suggest we do that, Sue?" Maya asked.

"There are sewerage tunnels that go all the way under the city. It might not be the nicest place to travel, but it would get you almost all the way to their location without being seen." She smiled. "That's our greatest advantage here. This is a human colony. We know it better than they do."

"But if they can sense us telepathically," Alexa said. "Why would being unseen in the sewers help?"

"They didn't sense us sneaking up at first," Maya said. "They only opened up their telepathic sense when I threw the pinecone things—when it was obvious somebody was around. I don't think they're constantly aware of everything around them. After all, we tune out a lot of auditory and visual information if we're not actively looking and listening."

"I also suspect their sense has a limited range, although we can't know for sure what that range is," Braxton said.

"Don't think, suspect, can't know for sure. I'm hearing a lot of uncertainty." Sue crossed her arms.

"Exactly," Braxton said. "This is only our second encounter with a completely alien species. We have to make some educated assumptions. Otherwise we'll be crippled by inaction and die anyway." He turned to Maya. "I like the plan."

"Right. Braxton, you're with me. We need our best soldier on point this time." She motioned toward Alexa. "Think you can put together some mines with a little advice from Braxton?"

"I just need to make sure I won't blow myself up. It won't be an extensive minefield, but I should be able to deal with any who get close to our camp."

"Fantastic. Another distraction at their camp would help."

"What about something natural?" Braxton asked.

An image of the stampeding animals she'd seen earlier flashed in Maya's mind. "I might be able to help with that. This planet has a population of indigenous animals. Big animals, the size of Earth cows. I saw them stampede after being chased by a big lizard thing."

Braxton frowned. "Do we have time to mess about with that?"

"Give me a way of scaring them, and I can give it a try," Sue said. "I'm not a lot of use for much else." She turned to Yintol. "Our alien friend can help me."

Yintol shuffled into the middle of the group. "I will help Sue. All of you, Dracnor are dangerous. Be careful."

"Dracnor? That's the name of the alien species out there?"

"Yes. Dracnor."

Maya nodded. "Okay. Let's kick some Dracnor butt."

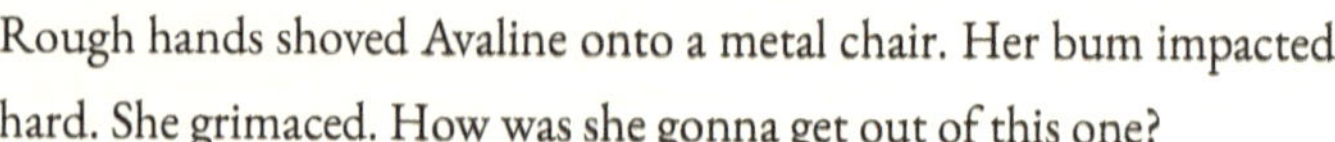

Rough hands shoved Avaline onto a metal chair. Her bum impacted hard. She grimaced. How was she gonna get out of this one?

Three men stared at her.

"What are you doing here?" It was the Kiwi who'd mugged her earlier.

"I came to get my stuff back."

The Kiwi scoffed. "You think I'm an idiot or something?"

Avaline chuckled humourlessly. "You really want me to answer that?"

"If you're hungry, you can go visit a restaurant. Nobody's gonna come down here after a basket of food. Specially not some pretty little girl like you."

Avaline gritted her teeth. Her hands formed into fists.

"I've taken down bigger men than you."

That had been in the courtroom, during her student work experience. But no need to mention that detail.

"It's just a basket of food. You risk coming down here by yourself for one basket of food, then you're the idiot."

Avaline took a slow breath and steeled herself. She locked eyes with the man. "It's not just food. I used a lot of rations for those supplies." Her voice hardened, razor-sharp. "It's my honeymoon."

"Oh well, congratulations. By all means, have the basket. Go celebrate with your hubby." The humour suddenly dropped from his face. "And why not tell security where to find us while you're at it" he yelled, millimetres from her face."

Kiwi rose up to full height and paced in front of her.

"What do we do with her?" the dark-skinned American man asked.

"We'll have to hold her here."

"How long? We can't keep her indefinitely."

"We'll have to figure that out, won't we. It's not like we can stay in here forever. If we did, they'd find us eventually."

So this was it. This was how her marriage would end. They were gonna kill her. It was written all over Kiwi's face. She took a rasping breath. *Till death do us part*. Not so romantic anymore. Daniel would be torn apart by this.

She never should have come here. Her heartbeat thrashed in her ears. Their marriage would end today, just because she wanted to make their honeymoon perfect. Odd that she'd think of the future of their marriage now. She hadn't thought much about the future lately. She'd been so focused on the present. On the honeymoon.

Wait! Her wristband could be tracked. They'd figure that out. She drew in a long slow breath. She didn't have to die today. Daniel would notice her absence, and she'd recorded that message for him. But how long would that take? Kiwi was on the edge. She might not have long. She scanned the room. Cargo containers lined the walls.

There were several doors leading out of the room. The one they'd come through was dead ahead. The catwalk hovered above it. Doors also waited to the left and right. Would they be locked? Maybe. She needed a distraction.

The three men here were still in enthusiastic discussion. This might be the closest they'd get to distracted. She rose and padded left. One step. Then another. Her rubber soles were virtually silent on the metal floor. They still hadn't noticed her. Any second now. She turned and sprinted for the door.

"Grab her!" Kiwi yelled. She bounded forward. Feet pounded behind her. Nearly there.

She reached the door. She grabbed the handle and pulled. Locked. Grep!

Arms grabbed her and dragged her back towards the chair.

"Stars, woman. You're fast."

Her legs went weak. She could barely walk as they dragged her back to the chair.

"Anyone think to take her wristband?" American asked.

"No." Kiwi grabbed her wrist.

"Ow." Pain ran up her arm. "You're hurting me."

Kiwi ripped the wristband off and threw it to the ground. "You're not calling for help." His heavy foot slammed onto the wristband, crushing it. Avaline cringed at the crunch of electronics.

"Tie her up," the American said.

A drop formed in the corner of Avaline's eye. She wasn't getting out of this, was she?

Maya grimaced and covered her nose. "Whew. I'd expected it to smell a bit down here, but nothing like this."

Braxton climbed down the ladder behind her and dropped onto the stone floor of the tunnel. "I dunno, Maya. I'd have expected it to be worse. I guess with modern processing technologies, it's not so bad."

Maya consulted a map, projected by her eye lenses. "Okay, so looks like we head this way." She pointed down a tunnel.

"Let's hope the walkways are still passable. I'd hate to have to wade through all that." Braxton pointed to the river of water and waste.

"You nervous?" Maya asked.

"You're always nervous before a battle. Never goes away, but I'm ready."

"You've faced the Dracnor before. You know how tough they are."

"So've you."

Maya chuckled. "I don't know if running for my life quite counts as 'facing them'."

"That was your job, to distract them. You weren't there to engage in battle. There was no shame in running."

They neared an intersection. Maya pointed to the right. Braxton took the lead.

"I just hope we pull this off," she said. "I really want to get back to the ship alive, for my daughter's sake."

"You have a daughter? How old?"

"Sixteen. Rotten age. She lives in your country, actually. My husband moved to Australia after our divorce. I was in the military, so was often offworld. Put too much pressure on our marriage. Crystal resented it even more than he did. I don't see much of her. I convinced her to come on this cruise so we could spend time together."

"That's nice."

Maya scoffed. "Yeah, well she's working as a child care assistant in the youth program. I still never get to see her. It's sad. I quit the military to spend more time with my family, but it was already too late. Guess I failed as a mother."

"Maybe, but the way I see it, this whole situation gives you a second chance. Think how lucky it is that your daughter was on *Jewel of The Stars* when the Dracnor took Earth. She's safe, and she's with you. That's what matters. It gives you a second chance."

"I guess it does."

"I'm not saying it's gonna be easy. Family is hard. Don't give up."

Maya nodded. They continued to walk in silence for another ten minutes before Maya stopped. "We're here. We have to go up this ladder."

Braxton started to climb. Maya took a deep breath. Ugh, what a mistake.

Seventeen

Jaylen looked up as Nari entered the office. She was alone.

"No Tyrell?"

"His wristband indicates he's in his stateroom, but he wasn't there. He must have taken it off and left it behind."

"Then he could be anywhere on the ship. We'll have to put out an old-fashioned APB." Jaylen reached for his wristband. The door slid open and a man ran in, taking gulps of air.

"Can I help you?"

"Yeah, she's missing." The man spoke with a British accent.

"Missing?"

"Yeah. Avaline. My wife. I think she's in trouble."

Jaylen smiled. "Maybe she's lost track of time in the casino. When was the last time you saw her."

"This morning. We made plans. We were going to have a picnic in our quarters, but she's not there. But that's not important."

"Calm down, sir. Take a deep breath and explain the situation."

"She sent me an email. Some thugs took her food, and she's gone after them. They might have hurt or killed her."

"Can I have your name, please?"

"Oh. Yeah. I'm Daniel. Daniel Barrett."

"And your wife's name?"

"Avaline Barrett."

Jaylen brought up a passenger manifest and swiped through it. "Here we are." He opened her record. "This is odd. Looks like she has two wristbands registered in her name."

"What? That doesn't sound right. She hates wristbands. Doesn't even like having one of them."

"The second one was registered just over an hour ago, here on the ship."

Daniel's eyes narrowed.

"I can't locate the new band. It's offline. Would she have turned it off, if she dislikes them so much?"

"No. She never turns it off, but she does sometimes stick it in her handbag.

"I'll try tracing the original band. A three-dimensional map appeared in Jaylen's field of vision. A dot indicated the location of the band. A cargo warehouse in the industrial section at the back of the ship. "It shouldn't be there."

"Where?"

"You said some people stole food from her?"

"Yes. I'll forward you the email."

Daniel swiped his hand and a notification appeared in Jaylen's field of view. He read it and turned to Nari. Could this be related to the Crimson Guard? Her eyes told him she was thinking the same thing.

Jaylen turned back to Daniel. "I need to go in and get her. I'm concerned she might be in danger."

"I'm coming with you."

"No. You wait here, Mr Barrett. I insist. I'll have somebody stay here with you."

Daniel's face paled, as much as his dark skin could.

Beep. Les swiped a notification. "Captain, Dalia Spring is here to see you," the second officer said.

That hadn't taken long. "Good. Send her in, please."

Les stood and circled around his desk to the door. Dalia Spring entered, again gesturing her entourage to remain outside.

"We should be having this discussion in my cabin rather than your office, Captain, but can I assume from this summons that you've come to your senses?"

"Would you like to take a seat?"

Spring sat.

Les sat opposite her, rather than behind his desk.

"Ms Spring. I've given a lot of thought to what you said. I understand your reasoning. I can see why you feel you should be in charge. Unfortunately, we're in a difficult situation, as we don't know if your purchase was completed before the aliens took control of Earth." He took a deep breath. *Here goes nothing.* "What it comes down to is this. I don't care."

Spring's face hardened. The lines became deeper. The space between her eyes contracted. She stared back at Les like an undersized bulldog.

"The status of the transaction doesn't matter to me. I'm not going to recognise your authority. This company, your bank account, they're all artefacts of an Earth that no longer exists. They're meaningless. If we were back on Earth, you wouldn't be one of the most powerful CEOs on the planet. You'd just be another subject of an occupying force. I'm afraid the rules have changed Ms Spring. This is my ship and I will remain in command."

Les clutched the armrests of his chair. He'd said his piece. How would Spring would react?

Her expression didn't change. She just continued to stare. Ten seconds. Twenty. Finally, she stood and locked eyes with Les.

"You've made a mistake, Captain."

"Perhaps, but if so, I'll live with it."

"There's a problem with your reasoning. If you choose to abandon to rules in this way, it means that you have to abandon all of them. Your authority on this ship becomes just as meaningless as mine. That means anarchy. I'm not sure you're prepared for that."

She strode toward the door. It slid open. "You've won this round, Captain, but this isn't over."

Eighteen

Maya climbed up out of the sewer. The forest was only about ten metres away. She sprinted forward into the cover, and Braxton followed. She ducked down and tapped her wristband.

"Maya to Alexa."

"Here."

"Report."

"I've managed to find a few sound recordings of dinosaurs and monsters from films in the stellarmesh cache. I don't know how similar they'll be to the predator creature you saw earlier. I've played a few sounds quietly. The herd is getting agitated. I'm pretty sure I can get them to stampede. I just hope they go in the right direction. With a little luck I should be able to herd them toward the Dracnor ship."

"Good." Braxton waved her forward. While she had greater authority on the ship, Braxton had held the higher military rank, and was more experienced in combat. He was the logical choice to lead this fight.

They ran forward in a crouched position, making the most of the forest's cover.

It didn't take long to reach the edge, where they could see the box-shaped ship. From this angle they could see two guards. The other

Dracnor soldiers must be near the shuttle by now. Hopefully Sue's mines would take them out.

Maya gripped her gun, her knuckles white. They had the advantage, hiding in the forest. Experience suggested the Dracnor used their claws as weapons. Did they even carry guns?

The ground rumbled, and a dull roar sounded. The stampede. Sue had done it. Maya looked up, listening intently. The noise was coming from the north-east. This was their chance. With a little luck, they wouldn't even need to fire a shot.

The Dracnor guard took a few steps forward, looking about. He had likely never seen the native animals. He wouldn't know what to expect. He? Was the alien male? Did the Dracnor have genders? There was so much they didn't know about their enemies.

The rumbling grew into a roar. Not long now. The Dracnor darted its head this way and that.

"Oh, grep," Braxton whispered. "Let me know if you smell cinnamon."

Maya's heart seized. The commotion would undoubtedly make the Dracnor reach out with their telepathic abilities. She and Braxton wouldn't stay hidden for much longer.

And there it was. Cinnamon. The telltale sign of Dracnor telepathy.

Maya took aim at the alien's head and fired. So much for surprise.

The Dracnor ducked. It reached behind its back and pulled out a black cylinder. It pointed the cylinder in Maya's direction. A weapon? She dove to the ground as a beam of blue fire burned through the air where her head had been.

She rose to her knees and fired off another shower of bullets.

Braxton's gun fired from the left.

Crash! The herd of alien animals bounded over the hill, running straight for the ship. The Dracnor turned toward them, distracted.

The herd veered east, running toward the clearing between the city and the forest. They wouldn't be trampling the Dracnor. Pity, but the distraction might be enough help.

Maya fired another round at the back of the Dracnor's head. A spray of bullets from Braxton's rifle hit the same spot. The alien shrieked.

Pain! The back of Maya's head stung with a thousand pinpricks. The smell of cinnamon was overpowering. She was feeling the Dracnor's pain. She fired again.

A beam of energy burst millimetres from her face. She dove. Twigs and pebbles bit into her arms and neck as she hit the ground. The other Dracnor guard. She'd forgotten all about him.

She rolled over. Braxton dropped the first guard with another spray of bullets.

Maya took aim at the second guard and fired. Braxton joined her. The alien fell backward. Together Maya and Braxton advanced, firing as they went.

The stampede was gone, the roar fading into the distance. The two Dracnor lay still.

"Don't assume they're dead," Braxton yelled. "I'm covering them but keep your weapon close."

"Got it." Maya slung her rifle over her shoulder, pulled out the cutting torch, and ran for the ship. She skidded to a stop and dropped to her knees. The metal was blackened and partially cut. Alexa had made good progress before they'd been forced to retreat. Maya ignited the torch and continued the cut. The beam from the torch sliced through the metal like scissors cutting paper.

Still no movement from the Dracnor guards. She was almost finished. Just another centimetre. Got it!

Maya grabbed the metal by the cool older cut, and tossed it away. The inside of the indentation was complicated—Lots of plastic tubes and lines printed on thermoplastic. There were no wires in sight.

There it was—a long cylindrical item with a bulge in the middle. That had to be the plasma coil.

She grabbed both ends and twisted. The coil came loose.

"Got it," she called out. She stuffed the coil into her backpack and gripped her gun.

A shriek. The first alien they'd gunned down leaped to its feet. Maya screamed and fired at the creature's head. Braxton sprayed bullets up and down the alien's body. It dropped, still.

Braxton turned to the second guard and repeated the process, shooting every part of the body. "Hopefully that'll prevent him from getting up, like his friend."

Maya tasted bile. Death. She hadn't tasted death in a long time. Years. These were Dracnor, but they were still intelligent life forms. Maya swallowed the bile. She was a soldier again. Time to be professional. She could indulge her conscience later.

"Braxton to Sue. We have the plasma coil. Heading back to the sewers."

Maya took one last look at the broken bodies of the aliens and followed Braxton back to the Sewer.

Nineteen

MAYA EMERGED FROM THE sewer tunnels and sprinted for the shuttle, Braxton's footsteps pounding behind her. She held her rifle at the ready, in case there were more Dracnor about.

She rounded a corner and neared the shuttle. All was quiet. Too quiet? She took a step forward, surveying her surroundings. Nothing. She approached the shuttle.

"Welcome."

Maya spun around. Yintol.

"Repairs well. Have you the coil?"

Maya tore her back-pack open and grabbed the plasma coil. She handed it to Yintol. He gripped it under one arm while scurrying toward the warp ring on his other five limbs.

Braxton chuckled, shaking his head. "Do you wonder how a species like that managed the technological advancement necessary to travel the stars? Their bodies don't seem to be built for it.

Maya nodded. "Just one of the mysteries behind our new friend. As long as he fixes the warp ring, I don't much care."

Maya strode over to the clearing in front of the shuttle, where they'd made all their plans. There could still be Dracnor out there.

Maya gasped. There was a body, just twenty metres away. Dracnor. It must have stepped on one of Alexa's mines.

"You should've seen it." Alexa leaned against the shuttle nursing a minor wound on her thigh.

"Are you sure it's dead?"

"Shot it a couple of times to make sure."

Maya turned to Braxton. "Think we should take it aboard?"

"I dunno, Maya. There are certainly benefits to studying their physiology, but it represents a potential risk."

"We know how to incapacitate them permanently."

Braxton nodded. "Give me a hand dragging him over."

Maya slung her gun over her shoulder and ran to the body. She gagged. Burnt flesh. Braxton took the right leg. Maya grabbed the left and heaved backward. The creature was lighter than expected. Maybe the explosion had reduced its overall mass. Maya grimaced. She'd never seen ground combat like this in her military days. Stars, it was gory. She should be able to handle this.

Another heave, and another. She glanced over her shoulder. Halfway there.

A beam of energy shot toward them. Pain tore through her upper left arm. She gasped and dropped the Dracnor's leg.

"Argh." Maya glanced at her arm. The beam had only grazed her, but stars, it was like fire.

"Alexa, cover us!" Braxton yelled. Gunfire sounded. In the distance, a Dracnor scurried to its left, dodging the bullets. "Come on, Maya. We can do this."

Maya gritted her teeth, grabbed the Dracnor's leg, and heaved again. Her heart pounded. Her arm burned. Sweat formed across her forehead and dripped into her eyes. Another beam fired. Something skidded in the gravel behind them. Another burst of gunfire. Maya glanced over her shoulder. Three more metres. Two. One. They dragged the alien up the ramp, into the cargo hold.

Braxton grabbed Maya's arm and tore off the charred remnants of her sleeve. "Looks like the beam cauterised the wound. It'll hurt like hell, but you're not gonna bleed to death."

Maya stepped outside and ducked around the corner as Yintol pressed a covering plate onto the warp ring.

"You done?" she asked.

"Finished," Yintol said.

"Everybody into the shuttle!"

Yintol squeezed himself through the doorway. Maya waved Braxton in. Alexa was retreating backwards toward the shuttle, still laying down fire.

Maya jumped inside. Sue was already at the controls.

"Engines firing. If this doesn't work, we'll blow ourselves apart. Either way, it'll be over soon."

Alexa dove backward into the shuttle. Maya mashed her fist onto the close button and the door slammed shut.

The floor rocked below her. She flailed for something to hold onto. Her hands found Braxton. Her stomach heaved. She closed her eyes, willing herself not to throw up. The shuttle burst forward.

Maya stood up straight and grabbed a hand strap.

The engine sputtered. The shuttle dropped. Maya's heart clenched, and her stomach jumped upward. They were falling.

The engine kicked in and the shuttle rose.

"Everyone okay back there?" Sue asked. "Engine's not in the best condition." She pressed a few controls. "Five hundred metres. Sorry about the rough ride. I haven't engaged inertial dampening yet. Fig-ured we should get off the ground quick as possible. Activating now."

The ride smoothed out a little.

"Accelerating to escape velocity … now." Sue swiped a control only she could see.

Maya stepped to the front of the shuttle and took her seat. Blue sky turned to black.

"We've achieved orbit," Sue said.

"Well?" Maya turned to face her.

"Course laid in for the agreed rendezvous coordinates."

Maya bit her lip.

"You realise that if the warp ring isn't repaired properly, this could go catastrophically wrong."

"We're aware of that, Sue. Please take us to warp."

Sue nodded and pressed the button.

The ship shook a little more violently than normal. The stars faded. An orb of white light appeared in the centre of the cockpit window.

They were at warp.

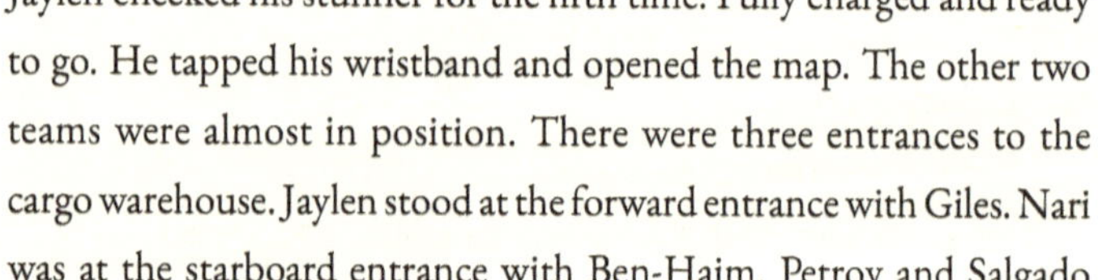

Jaylen checked his stunner for the fifth time. Fully charged and ready to go. He tapped his wristband and opened the map. The other two teams were almost in position. There were three entrances to the cargo warehouse. Jaylen stood at the forward entrance with Giles. Nari was at the starboard entrance with Ben-Haim. Petrov and Salgado approached the port entrance. With Maaka dead and Alexa off the ship, this was his entire security team. Plenty for a normal cruise, but woefully inadequate for their current situation.

There was no telling what they'd find in the warehouse. If only the surveillance cameras were working. The kidnappers must have disabled them. The positive aspect was the kidnappers couldn't see them coming. The map showed no wristband signals, so they'd obviously disabled them. Who knew how many people waited in there for them?

"Petrov to Banks."

Jaylen swiped the notification. "Banks here."

"We're in position."

"All right. On three. One … two … three."

Jaylen flung the door open and ran in, stunner outstretched. "Security! Nobody move."

Tyrell Armstrong and Aiden Harris stood in the centre of the room. Near them, a young woman sat tied to a chair. The men drew stunners and opened fire. Jaylen dove out of the way of the electric bolt and fired one of his own. Tyrell ducked behind a cargo container. Both bolts were absorbed by the bulkheads.

The port and starboard teams moved in, firing their stunners.

Bolts of light flew in both directions from above Jaylen's head. He looked up. There was another man on a catwalk above his head. He looked back down. Nari and Petrov were both unconscious.

Jaylen dove out into the middle of the room, twisting around as he aimed at the catwalk. He fired. His bolt clanged on a metal support beam, millimetres from his target.

The lights went out. Complete blackness. Jaylen's breathing quickened. What now? He couldn't shoot what he couldn't see. Feet scurried across the metal floor to his left. Zap. Another bolt. Thump. A body hitting the deck.

Of course! Night vision. Jaylen tapped his wristband and scanned the menu for the night vision option. It was in there somewhere. There. He jabbed his finger at the icon. The room flooded with green light. Tyrell Armstrong and Aiden Harris lay on the floor, out cold.

He looked up. The catwalk was empty. Salgado was down.

"Sir?" Ben-Haim asked.

"Go after them."

Ben-Haim nodded and ran for the port door. Jaylen skidded over to the chair.

"Avaline Barrett?"

"Yes," the woman said in a tight British accent.

"Your husband reported you missing. You're safe now."

She let out a shaky laugh.

"Can you tell me anything about the kidnappers?" He untied her hands.

Avaline closed her eyes and nodded several times. "One of them was from New Zealand. He was the tall one. The other two were both American. They said something about a Crimson Guard."

Jaylen nodded. "I've had some dealings with them over the last two days." Jaylen pulled the binds free from Avaline's hands. She gripped his wrist. "Don't worry. We'll have you reunited with Daniel as soon as the Doctor checks you over."

Avaline smiled.

His wristband beeped with another notification. *"Ben-Haim to Banks."*

Jaylen swiped it. "Go ahead."

"I've lost him, sir. The third one disappeared into the depths of the ship. With no wristband, I can't track him."

"Then report back here." Jaylen surveyed the room. "We've got some clean-up to do."

Twenty

"I WANT TO KNOW who else is involved in this Crimson Guard." Jaylen locked eyes with Tyrell Armstrong.

"I don't know what you're talking about."

"Your girlfriend has already admitted to being part of it all."

Tyrell's face clouded.

"You know what I think? I think you used your charm to get friendly with her, knowing she had access to food stores at the restaurant. I think you convinced her to let you in and act surprised."

Tyrell's eyes went wide.

"So either tell me who you report to, or I'll have to assume you're the ringleader."

"It wasn't like that."

Jaylen leaned back in his chair. "Then tell me how it was like."

"I didn't get friendly with her. She got friendly with me. The whole thing was her idea. It was obvious I was partial to the ladies. I mean, nobody can resist those French girls, right, brother?"

"So you're saying Brigitte is your only link to the organisation."

"I swear it on my life."

Jaylen stood. "Time to take a break. I'll have Nari take you to the holding cell."

Jaylen left the interview room, walked into the security office, and nodded to Nari. "Can you take him back to the brig?"

"No problem. But before I do, I just got word." Her face dropped.

"What is it?"

"While we were storming the storage bay and rescuing Avaline, our main food stores were raided."

Jaylen's gut turned to stone. "How much did they get?"

"Enough to feed a couple of people for months if they ration it well."

"We've been played." Jaylen shook his head. "They probably set up Tyrell, Brigitte, and Aiden to be the fall guys all along to throw us off the scent of what the Crimson Guard were really doing. That's why they made a thing of announcing their name."

"We couldn't have known. Like you said, we're not cops, even with your prior experience. We're just cruise ship security."

"We're gonna have to become more than that, Nari. Much more. But I promise you this. It's the last time these people make a fool of me."

◄O►

Maya gripped the armrest of her seat. Lights flickered in the shuttle. The engines groaned and sputtered.

"That doesn't sound good, Sue."

"Shuttle, this is *Jewel of The Stars*." A voice came through the comm channel. "You are cleared for docking in the aft shuttle bay."

"Roger that, *Jewel*," Sue said. "Don't panic, Maya, almost there. I'll get us in."

"See that you do."

The ship jolted in through the shuttle bay doors, and Sue eased them down onto the deck. Maya leaned back in her seat and closed her eyes. Thank goodness that was over.

She stood and surveyed her crew. They could all use a day off. Yintol was still clinging to any handhold he could find with all six limbs. How would the captain respond to their new friend? Only one way to find out.

"Yintol, remain here in the shuttle a moment."

"I will remain."

"Everyone else, move out. You've done incredibly well. I'm sure we can spare a few stewards to help unload the cargo."

The door opened. Braxton and Alexa filed out. Maya followed. Captain Miller stood off to the side.

"Congratulations, Maya. A job well done. I hear you brought back everything you set out to find."

"Yes, Captain, and a little something extra as well."

"Oh?" Miller raised an eyebrow.

"We ran into the aliens on the planet. They shot us down. We almost didn't get away, but we had some help."

"From whom?"

"Well," she fidgeted with her hands. "I'd like you to meet Yintol." She looked over her shoulder. "Come out, Yintol."

The alien ambled out of the ship on all six, slower than Maya would have liked. Miller gasped.

"Maya, what is that?"

"He's a friend. He was shot down by the aliens."

"He *is* an alien."

"He's a Nilf. The aliens who invaded Earth are called the Dracnor."

Miller stepped forward and put out his hand like a stop signal. "That's quite far enough, Mr Yintol."

Yintol stopped and regarded Miller. What was going through the creature's mind?

"I think it best he waits inside the shuttle."

Yintol nodded, turned, and retreated.

Miller glared at Maya. "What were you thinking?"

"Without him, we'd never have gotten off that planet alive."

"You've brought an alien on board my ship."

"Yes. A friendly alien. He's not a Dracnor, Captain."

Miller crossed his arms. "I have to think about this. You should have consulted me."

"There was no time. We were under attack and most of the shuttle's systems were down. That included comms." Maya bit her lip. "And I suppose I'd better mention the Dracnor body we brought back for Doctor Clark to study."

Miller regarded her with a stony expression. "Nobody leave," he called out. "I'm going to need the doctor to clear everyone in this room of biocontamination before you can rejoin the ship's population."

"Is that really necessary?" Maya asked.

"It's that or a three-day quarantine. And I'm including myself in this as well." Miller gestured toward the shuttle. "As for your new friend, I'm not about to let an alien walk free on this ship. Can you imagine the panic it will cause? People have been through a terrible ordeal and they're looking for someone to blame."

"Yintol isn't to blame."

"I'm sure that's true, but do you really think that will matter? No. For the moment, he'll remain on the shuttle until I decide what to do with him."

"Captain, you can't—"

"It's as much for his protection as ours."

Maya nodded slowly.

Jaylen dropped into his chair. His private cubicle in the security office was silent save for the ambient growl of the engines. He buried his face in his hands, elbows on the desk before him.

The Crimson Guard was still out there. Sure, he had Brigitte and Tyrell in custody, but they were just the tip of a cancerous iceberg. People were scared. It made sense that they'd band together and look out for their own interests, but something like this? It had arisen so quickly. Something deliberate was behind this. Somebody had a plan, and it was about more than stockpiling food. It wasn't going to fade away now Maya had brought back additional food supplies.

At least they'd returned Avaline Barrett safely to her husband. If anyone deserved to have a nice happy life here on the ship, it was people like them. They should be heading back to Earth to begin their new life together, not fighting for their lives out here.

Jaylen scrolled through Avaline's profile. She was a lawyer. That could be handy if Captain Miller wanted to hold trials. Of course, in this case, Avaline was also the victim.

"Sir?" Nari's voice.

Jaylen turned. "What's up?"

"Just wanted to let you know that our third kidnapper has been identified. Wayne Hill. Seems he's abandoned his stateroom on Deck ten. No personal belongings in there. He even took the pillowcases.

"I almost had him, Nari."

"Don't worry. We'll catch him. There's only so many places to hide on this ship."

"I guess."

A notification popped up in Jaylen's field of vision. He swiped it into the centre of his view. A text email.

Howdy, Chief Banks. Nice catching up with you today. Clever of Mrs Barrett having a second wristband hidden in her food basket. Guess you caught a lucky break. Nice job getting Dubois, Harris, and Armstrong. You can have them for free. Justice will be served. But I must warn you to drop this case. You can't stop us. Just leave us alone, and let nature take its course.

Crimson Guard.

"He's toying with us." Jaylen swiped the email over to Nari's contact icon.

Nari nodded slowly.

"Can you get a trace on that message?"

"No problem." She poked a few invisible controls. "Ah, Chief ..."

"Yeah?"

"The message. It came from ... you."

Jaylen crossed his arms. "Clever."

"They've told us one thing."

"Somebody in the Crimson Guard has quite the talent for hacking our computer network."

"Can't be too many like that on board."

Jaylen smiled. "This isn't over."

❖

Avaline closed her eyes and lay her head on Daniel's chest. Daniel's fingers stroked her back.

"Do you think we'll ever get sick of doing that?" she asked.

"I hope not."

"You know the best thing about getting stuck on this ship for the rest of our lives?"

"What's that?"

"We get to be together forever."

Daniel kissed her forehead. "That sounds good. Assuming, of course, that you don't run off and try to take on anymore organised crime gangs by yourself."

Avaline chuckled. "Don't worry. Once was more than enough." She leaned up on her left elbow. "I'm sorry I was so stupid."

"You weren't the only one. I can't believe I stayed away all night. A bottle is a poor companion. Especially when you have a hot wife waiting back home."

Avaline sat up. I guess we should put some clothes on and get a little dinner."

"Yes, we should." Daniel climbed out of the bed. "We should make this special somehow. Tonight is the last official night of the cruise. We were supposed to disembark back on Earth tomorrow morning."

Avaline shrugged. "Doesn't matter. It's just a date on a calendar." She stood and put her arms around Daniel. "From now on, I want to make every night special."

"You've changed your tune." Daniel put his arms around her.

"I got thinking. After the honeymoon comes the marriage, and I'm looking forward to making that long and happy."

"Glad to hear it," Daniel stepped out of the embrace. Avaline tried to pull him back in but he'd already turned around.

"Thing is though, they're putting on another show tonight." He bent over to pick up his shirt. "The grand finale. Celebrating the end of the cruise. We don't want to miss that."

Avaline crossed her arms. "There'll be other shows. The performers aren't going anywhere. Besides. I have a better idea."

Daniel turned and smiled. "Didn't we just do that?"

Avaline picked up her shirt and mock hit him with it. "Not that." They both laughed. "I was thinking we could offer to watch Ronald Scott's kids for him, so he can go to the show."

Daniel's eyes went wide.

"He's trying to take care of them alone while his wife is in a coma. He could use a night off, and the captain has granted most of the crew the night off. That means no babysitters."

"Avaline Barrett, you continue to amaze me." He took her right hand and stroked it.

"It'll be fun. Get in a little practice." She buttoned Daniel's shirt for him. "Get us ready for the day when we have kids of our own."

"Sounds great."

Avaline stepped in closer and kissed him.

Epilogue

Morris Perino adjusted his tie and opened the heavy metal door. This part of the ship was so dreary. A man glanced nervously toward him.

"Relax." Morris closed the door.

"It's you," Wayne Hill said.

"I bring a message from my employer. You've done well. You caused quite the disruption over the last two days."

"But we lost three of our number."

Morris shrugged. "That's of no consequence."

"What about the consequences to me? I can't go back to my cabin. I'm a fugitive, and there are only so many places on this ship I can hide. I can't use any ship services. I'll have to steal every meal I eat."

"My associates will take care of you. Don't worry."

"They'd better. I put everything on the line for your associates."

"You probably feel like a caged animal right now, but that won't last. Things are going to change on this ship. The captain's dynasty will soon end."

"Good. Nice to know we're on the winning side."

Morris nodded. He handed Wayne a slip of paper. Hard to come by, but useful for clandestine activities. "This is a safe area. Food will be provided daily."

Hill nodded.

"I'll take my leave now."

Morris turned and pulled the heavy door open. He strode through the hallway and emerged back into the main passenger area of the ship. He took the stairs up one level and pressed the door chime on one of the luxury staterooms. The door slid open.

Morris padded inside. A desk chair faced away from him. Its occupant didn't turn. "It's done. I gave him the coordinates. He's headed there now." He shifted his weight to the other foot. "Should I alert security to his location and end this?"

"No," a female voice said from the chair. "The captain is not being cooperative. We may have need for the Crimson Guard in the future. Keep them around, but quiet for now."

The chair swung around, dwarfing its occupant.

Morris nodded. "As you wish, Ms Spring."

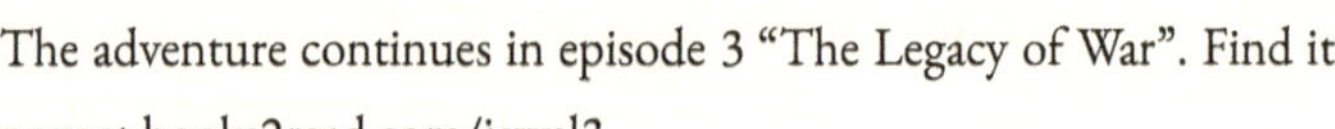

The adventure continues in episode 3 "The Legacy of War". Find it now at books2read.com/jewel3

The Adventure Continues

To be sure you hear of future releases, sign up to my email list. Not only will you get monthly updates, but you'll also receive the free prequel story that explains first contact between humans and the Dracnor.

Join today at

www.adamdavidcollings.com/free

If you enjoyed this story, please leave a review wherever you purchased it from. Reviews are the lifeblood of authors.

Acknowledgments

Firstly, I want to say a big thank you to my very patient readers. I made you wait a lot longer for this second episode than I should have. It took a lot to whip this particular story into shape, and things were set back when the engine of my car blew up, and I had to use the money I'd saved for publishing this book to get it towed home for scrap.

But I persevered, and here we are.

Thank you to my editor, Iola Goulton for your expertise and wisdom.

Thank you to my cover designer, Domi (Inspired Cover Designs), for working your magic and once again turning a scene from my head into a beautiful image.

Thank you to my fellow writers in the Realm Makers Consortium and Omega Writers. What wonderful supportive communities we have.

Thank you to my parents for continuing to believe in my dreams and encouraging me to pursue them.

Thank you to my wife and children. Every author knows that the creation of a book is impossible without the love and support of family. You are as much a part of this project as I am. I love you.

And thank you to God, who gifted me with a passion for writing. May your Holy Spirit continue to move me to write stories that are worth telling.

Adam David Collings.

October 2019.

Also By Adam David Collings

Jewel of The Stars

Episode 1 "Earth's Remnant"

Episode 2 "A New Reality"

Episode 3 "The Legacy of War"

The Christmas Star Disaster

Short Stories in Anthologies

Medieval Mars

Glimpses of Light

The Crossover Alliance Anthology "Superheroes"

Challenge Accepted – A Charity Anthology

Find them at AdamDavidCollings.com/books

About Author

Adam David Collings is an author of speculative fiction. He lives in Tasmania, Australia with his wife Linda and his two teenage children. Adam draws inspiration for his stories from his over-active imagination, his life experiences and his faith.

Adam is a great lover of stories and is the host of the Nerd Heaven podcast where he discusses sci-fi and fantasy from TV, film, and books. You can also find these discussions on youTube.

With his family, Adam produces a travel vlog called The Collings Show, sharing the sights of Tasmania and beyond.

Somehow, amongst all these creative endeavours, family time, and church, Adam finds time to have a day job as a software developer.

Find links to all his content at AdamDavidCollings.com